CORPORATE GIRLS

VOLUME I

A Novel By: Tawana Necole

Corporate Chics: Volume I

This book is a work of fiction. Names, characters, places, and incidents were creatively written and are products of the author's imagination.

Printed in the United States of America

First Printing, 2009

Second Printing, 2015

ISBN 978-1-943284-02-3 (pbk.)

ISBN 978-1-943284-03-0 (ebk)

Library of Congress Control Number: 2015906221

A2Z Books Publishing
1990 Young Rd
Lithonia, GA 30058

www.A2ZBooksPublishing.com

Cover Illustrator- Jerron Leary

Manufactured in the United States of America

10 9 8 7 6 5 4 3 2

Gibbs, Tawana Necole Corporate Chics / by Tawana Necole.

paperback ed. p. cm.1. Corporate Chics---Fiction. 2. USA Investment Firm---Fiction. 3. Atlanta (ATL)---Fiction. 4. College Life---Fiction. 5. Savannah, GA---Fiction.

For information about special discounts for bulk purchase, please contact Corporate Chics Enterprises with *Sales* in the subject line at TawanaNecole@CorporateChics.net.

Tawana Necole is available for speaking engagements. For more information or to book for an event contact Corporate Chics Enterprises via the contact page at www.CorporateChics.net

Corporate Chics *are women who are courageous, unstoppable, inspirational, encouraging, and empowering. She doesn't necessarily have to work in the corporate world but she is definitely about business. This is a movement of females who believe in living a life of quality and if you believe that you are any of the adjectives in the first sentence...she is you, you are her, and we are* **Corporate Chics.**

In Memory of Byron Brown, Parnell Johnson, Ellen Coaxum, Maggie Snipe, Wendell Simmons, Joann Howard, Arthur Simmons, Cleveland Coaxum, Sr., and to all those who lost a loved one way to soon.

Introduction

...a preliminary part, as of a book, musical composition, or the like, leading up to the main part

I knew this had to be done…and there was no turning back. The decision was made and no matter how much I didn't want to do this, I was stuck with the consequences of my actions, *again*. As I am sitting in church, I heard God speaking directly to me and my situation. The more the Preacher preached, the more the tears flowed. The people that were sitting next to me started looking at me with the *concern* eye. One of them tapped an usher on the shoulder and pointed at me. Sure enough the old lady came over in her stiff red suit and pushed a box of Kleenex in my face. I gave her a stern look and grabbed about ten pieces of tissue and dared her to say something to me. Questions were the only thoughts flooding my mind.

How did this happen again?

Why is it so easy for me to make such a difficult, sacrificial decision?

How did I end up in the same place within five years?

As the Preacher continued to say over and over how much God loved me, I didn't believe it. In that moment, it felt like he was speaking directly to me.

Just two weeks ago, I was in Pin-ups, which is a raggedy ass strip club on the east side of Atlanta, asking a dancer about possibly having a threesome with Vegas. It was one of our fantasies and I was determined to live it out this year. We talked about it the first year we hooked up but never acted on it. Crazy thing about it; I was with my side piece, Troy, for his thirtieth birthday. Troy's birthday was seven days before Vegas' birthday. We had it all planned out. Vegas and I were fussing and arguing since he looked in my phone and found the private text messages to Troy. So Troy and I had to be slick and undercover. The thing about Atlanta, is that it is really big, but then really small at the same time. Getting lost in Buckhead or even Alpharetta was super easy. Black folks weren't coming to those places on a regular day. Places like that were for the celebrities, the elite and the gays… Black folks only came to this part of town for special occasions (birthdays, holidays, and tax money season.) If a cheater wanted to get caught, the quickest way was to go to Midtown, College Park, Camp Creek or Decatur. Anywhere, where most of the middle-classed, ghetto-working folks lived, I had to stay far away from. Or someone that we went to college with would have seen me.

So everything was set. It was the middle of a work week and I only worked a half day so we could meet in a neutral place. I don't know what he told his wife or how he was able to get away from her and their three kids, but he pulled it off. He told me he was unhappy and the decision for them to separate was definitely mutual. He told me all the bull shit that most married men tell their side piece and I really believed him. We were in-sync in every way and he trusted me and I trusted him. We met at Pin-Ups; it was the closest place to us. The day-before, I went to take out a Title Max loan on my car, because my money was still tied up with all of the bull shit Vegas got us into and I needed money. I received about a $7500 check and spent $1000 just in Pin-Ups alone.

As I am whispering in *Brown Sugars'* ear asking her how it works when it came to putting together a threesome; Troy is watching me with the green envious eye. Of course I couldn't let him know that I was planning to have a *ménage a trois* that did not involve him. I felt guilty about Vegas finding out about my affair with Troy and I had to do something to win back his love. Although Vegas caused this on himself and did nothing to claim me as his, our actions began to reciprocate. I did what he was doing and he was the reason I didn't want to commit. My intuition had me convinced that he was cheating on me and I was tired of being a good girl when it came to him.

Vegas was super mysterious and smart about his cheating ways and his bitches were trained. If they knew about me, they weren't bold enough to admit it. Vegas hid his phone in his sneakers and because he had almost every pair of Jordan's created, it was hard to check every shoe without waking him in the middle of the night or when he took showers. This man would take his SIM card out of his phone (this was before the iPhone became popular) replace it with a dummy SIM card and then hide the phone in a totally different shoe. If I did manage to find both, I couldn't break his code. There were times I would try and trick him into telling me the truth. I would call him in the middle of the day while at work, demanding that he tell me about the chic that called me on my job. Of course that didn't happen but he fell for it twice and I still couldn't get the truth out of him, because about two minutes into the conversation he knew I was lying. If I wasn't snooping around in his closet or trying to trick him with the fake "oh your bitch called my job!" hoax, I was on the computer hacking and breaking into his email. I was determined to get the truth. But he was the best at hiding t*he truth* from me. He never wanted me to know what he was doing. Plus, he knew better then to have a bitch knocking at my pent house door asking me, "Who are you?" My brother used to tell me that he lied to the girls that he loved and I would understand that statement one day. I told him that was the stupidest thing I ever heard of in my life. I could no longer take the stares and the many thoughts that kept pouring into my mind based on the sins that I committed over the last three months, so I placed one finger in air and exited the church.

Reputation & Character

The circumstance amid which you live determines your reputation; **the truth you believe determines your character.**

Reputation is what you are supposed to be, **character is what you are.**

Reputation is a manufactured thing rolled and plated and hammered and brazed and bolted; **character is growth.**

Reputation comes over one from without; **character grows from within.**

Reputation is what you have when you come into a new community; **character is what you have when you go away.**

Your reputation is earned in an hour; **your character does not come into light for a year.**

Reputation is made in a moment; **character is built in a lifetime.**

Reputation grows like a mushroom; **character lasts like eternity.**

A single newspaper report gives you your reputation; **a life of toil gives you your character.**

If you want to get a position, you need reputation; **if you want to keep it, you need character.**

Reputation makes you rich or makes you poor; **character makes you happy or makes you miserable.**

Reputation is what men say about you on your tombstone; **character is what the angels say about you before the throne of God.**

Reputation is the basis of the temporal judgment of men; **character is the basis of the eternal judgment of God.**

William Hersey Davis

Chapter 1:
College Days ~ Graduate

"I was learning that most new relationships are unpredictable despite how wonderful they can seem in the beginning. A lasting alliance can only happen when you have two focused and committed partners." **-Omar Tyree**

Vegas then started to say, *"I prayed that you and I could be alone together for just five minutes."* ~ **Vegas**

When I saw him, I didn't see him because I knew what he was all about and I wasn't trying to go down that road with anyone else. But guys seem to think that "no" really means "yes." I guess it's a MAN LAW or something because he was very persistent. Vegas and his partners were some fun, spending-money type guys that were always trying to hook up with me and my friends. But we only saw them as that: fun, spending-money type guys. Our favorite slogan; "I ain't saying I'm a gold digger, but I ain't fucking with a broke nigga." We weren't trying to get in a relationship with any of them. Well, I'll say we acted like we didn't want to get in a relationship with any of them. The college chics I hung out with were all sneaky and secretive. But we watched each other's back. You never knew who was probably messing around with Vegas or his friends, but we played it cool when we all would hang out. And when we hung out, it was literally like the club scenes in the music videos. Shots, blunts, and fun was being had.

Austin Goodyear a.k.a. Vegas had beautiful caramel skin that matched perfectly with his beautiful dark brown eyes. He is a tall slender guy; I'll say about 6'1' and the waves in his hair made girls drool. I knew him but didn't officially meet him until the summer before my senior year of college. He was definitely one of the guys that the chics in Savannah would talk about.

Broughton Street & River Street was the place to be on Thursday and Friday nights for college students. Many people didn't have Friday classes, so Thursday was the official start of the weekend. My home girls and I went in on the "green" (translation the weed) & the drinks and OMG I loved the feeling that I would get when I was high. I didn't have a care in the world and my alter-ego, Kiki was born every time. I was never courageous enough to mess with anything like cocaine or ecstasy pills, because I wasn't trying to get addicted to N-E-thing. Ann, my mother, would have to be admitted to a psychiatric ward if I ever got strung out, so I didn't play around with man-made drugs. But I was a functional pot-smoker for a very long time.

"You only live once" is my motto. So live life to the fullest- **cautiously**. Meaning, have fun but don't sleep with every guy that comes into your world or has some type of interest in you; don't spend all your money on clothes and weed and when it's time to pay the rent, you are broke. That is super ghetto. So that's where the cautious part comes into play.

Austin and his friends would buy out the bar and then post-up in VIP. If we knew they were going out, we would be sure to make sure Val had the scoop on where. Val was from Atlanta and was cool with every type of dude on campus. She knew the nerds because she was a biology major; she knew the weed smokers because she loved to smoke but would never contribute; she knew the dope boys because she was their go-to girl when they were trying to get with the pretty girls; and she knew the white boys because they loved being around her; she was hilarious and kept them in-the-know about everything Black. Once Val told us where they were hanging out, she would let us know so we could just so happen to show up. We would show up, get in free, drink for free and meet up at a late night restaurant and eat for free. Ladies, you know we love free. Especially a free meal after the club when you are wasted and high with the munchies. I was straight when it came to money while in college but if I didn't have to spend my own, I didn't. These dudes used to "ball" out of control in Frozen Paradise, Après, Congo, and Oz. The streets had this story going about Austin and his friends. They didn't hustle or sell drugs, but they were stick-up boys; out–of-town thieves. They were always going out of town for something, but we never knew what that something was. They would leave in one car and come back in another with bags of cash. Assumptions had everyone speculating about their lifestyle. I don't know how true this was, but that's what they said. Whoever the hell they were, knew something because that very same rumor came to tear my life apart.

Although I didn't know or care what Vegas and his friends were doing (at that time) I did know this: they would gamble and bet BIG money. These dudes would bet on the Madden Play Station game, football games, boxing fights, spades, dice games and the list goes on and on and on. WTF? Who would want to lose money to that type of shit, because at the end of the day, somebody was going to lose big. I guess it's another MAN LAW that I don't understand. But, that's how Mr. Austin Goodyear got the nickname Vegas. Not because he didn't mind taking the risk gambling, but because he was always winning.

Never committed to one person, Vegas was the most available bachelor at the school. Don't get it twisted; we weren't the only females Vegas and his friends would show a good time. One of the most important things I have learned about a young, single, straight, guy is - he's gonna chase the cat! We all know females jump-quick to try and claim a man and the title. But no one could do this with him. He was the shit and knew it didn't stink. Something about him made me very curious. I would always catch him watching me or being extra nice. At first I didn't pay any attention to it, but his persistence made me want to know more about him. I began to have a crazy crush on him in the worst kind of way. Although, he never knew I felt this way, he did know I was the queen of playing hard to catch.

One thing about "wanting" someone is that you never know what you are getting when you do get what you think you want. Dealing with a bad boy is a world of trouble. You see how fast J-Lo left Diddy after that situation where someone was shot in the club? For some odd reason, I was always attracted to them. Mary J. Blige calls him Mr. Wrong. I am not trying to justify this but I loves me a bad boy. A rebel; you know the guys that create their own rules. The guys with 100% swag...

Because I was attracted to that type of person, my actions and my choices were influenced by him and his decisions. Something about an aggressive man, made me extremely curious. Deep down in my heart, I used to think that I could be the one to change him. That false hope kept me taking the same test over and over and over again. It took forever for me to realize that change is the only constant in life. I wasn't mature enough back then to know everything I wanted, I wasn't supposed to have. Ann, tried to teach it to me, but I made my own rules too. One important life lesson, that I will never forget is when people develop and mature, they must change in their development process. Unfortunately, I had to learn the hard way. I had to take the trial and error road. I guess the saying is true: "Trials & tribulation is something no one can hide from." And most times, we suffer because of our own unwise choices.

I know God will not give me anything I can't handle. I just wish that He didn't trust me so much. -**Mother Teresa**

Senior Year '03

It was my senior year when I finally allowed curiosity to get the best of me. The more we hung out with the bad boys on campus, the more I got to know him. Although I never gave him my phone number, he would make it his business to corner me and throw hints about himself through small conversations. I knew his government name (middle name included-*Austin Ronald Goodyear*) and partial life story. The perception that he portrayed was not who he was. It was so misleading, all negative, and basically untrue.

I eventually found out the truth when I started working for the Investment Firm. It seemed like he always felt the need to please his friends. Bill Cosby said it best: "*I don't know the key to success, but the key to failure is trying to please everybody*" and that was Mr. Vegas' problem. Because Ann taught me to master the art of observing, I noticed that Vegas was not like many of the guys in our age range but people pleasing was his forte.

Vegas did everything with his ~~friends,~~ I mean homeboys. He said he didn't have friends. I would always tell him, you sure could fool me. I guess some men just like to shoot the breeze (you know talk shit about women and man stuff). They love to kick it with their male counterparts (see who could win the-who-knows-the- most-about-*whatever* argument). A*nother* MANLAW… But in my book, homeboys are always going to be homeboys. They are cool to kick it or have fun with, but when it comes down to making life-altering decisions that involves deep

18

soul searching, you cannot depend on them solely for advice. Down the road of life, Vegas would learn the hard way about these so-called friends. Crazy as it is, hindsight and experiences has always been the story of our lives.

In the spring prior to my senior year, I won the title, Miss Savannah State University. That same semester, Vegas jumped a S-Class Benz; pearl white to be exact, and *that* is what really caught my eye. The Homecoming parade was right around the corner so I needed something classy and sexy to distinguish me from the other chic's in the parade. I didn't want to ride on a big bulky float with the runner-ups. Remember I made the rules?

So, I went straight to his apartment and knocked on the door. It was about ten o'clock on a Saturday morning. I was nervous praying that one of his chicken heads didn't answer the door. I was extremely shy whenever I had to deal with him one-on-one and the fact that I had a crush on him made my nerves even worse. Damn, how I wish I could be *Kiki* anytime and anyplace without the help of weed.

I took my planner and tablet because this was business. When he came to the door, he couldn't believe I was standing at his doorstep. I have always been persistent but polished in the way I went about business and the things I wanted. (I guess Vegas and I were more alike than different.) Vegas knew the cool, chill, fun side of Koilya, but not this side. I didn't want to come off as desperate or too anxious. So many thoughts were flooding my mind as I was walking to the door. "How can I help you Miss Lady" is actually what he said after I finally built up enough nerve to knock on the door. While I was checking out his place, I replied, "Good Morning, Vegas. Were you asleep?" "Naw. What's good shawty?" He replied. "I need to be represented in a classy and sophisticated way; can you help me with that?"

Now his apartment was just like him: Fresh and oh so clean… Of course he had what a man could never do without; a Big Screen T.V! Ladies, you know all real men must have a flat screen television. Watching sports is just so much better in HD. All of his furniture came from Bova; a modern furniture store in Atlanta. Now, some college dudes may have had a decent car with rims or radio system, but never an S-Class Benz and super laid apartment. Once I saw his apartment, I upgraded Vegas to "White-boy" status. Beyonce was wrong about this one. He was already upgraded!

I know I sound like a gold digger, but don't judge me because I like love nice things. My theory was this: in order to not have too many worries, money is a necessity in life and in relationships. Point. Blank. Period. I know that happiness should come first, but for argument sake, ask someone who is financially secure and someone opposite. When people lack money or don't have enough of it, life is hard. Living paycheck to paycheck isn't really living. I'd rather argue with my spouse about cooking, not in-sufficient funds and overdraft fees. In order to take care of me, my needs, and my wants, money has to be in the equation. Think about the economy and how fucked up it was for almost five years before President Obama came in and rescued us! Being able to maintain my bills and experience life without any financial worries is important to me. I am not a complacent type of chic. Investing and making money work for me/not me working for money; was my formula. But *life had a huge surprise for me?*

"I prayed for this very moment" is what he said."
I said, "Excuse me?" while I got my thoughts together.
Vegas then started to say, "I prayed that you and I could be alone together for just five minutes." I was thinking to myself, *Come on now with the extra sensitive pimp lines.*

"Vegas I only came here today to ask you if you wanted to place your car in the parade. Miss SSU needs a distinguished look" is how I responded. "That's cool Koilya, but curiosity drew you to me, plus you already said that. I know you are Miss SSU." "Austin," I started as soon as the U left his lips, "Did you want to place your car in the Homecoming parade or not? That's a yes or no question." Vegas then said, "Koilya, did you not hear me? Or are you so intrigued that you're edgy and the nervousness is turning into aggressiveness and control? I am not used to seeing you buckle under pressure Miss Lady." He took a sip of his apple juice. I did a double take. WTF! I wasn't prepared for this...
He was trying to get all in my head. Especially, with the way he was talking.

I didn't know he knew big words! I had to regain control of the conversation ASAP! Oh, how I wished I played my cool card in this situation by not going to his house. But you live and you learn... "Austin, I apologize that my energy takes your breath away. I really didn't know that I could have that effect on a guy like you. I guess that's why you are motivated to kick your best pimp lines. But today you don't have to waste your breath or your time. Thank you for being so cool, like you always are. Here are my digits and email address so I know we will be in contact about this arrangement. Thank you so much once again and enjoy your day sweetie."

I walked off with a soft smile on my face so he wouldn't have an opportunity to respond. A twitch was in my walk but I didn't want him to think I was being a smart ass. My smile was stern but extra cheesy and I waved a cute princess wave just as I was about to get into my car. He responded, "Aight Miss Koilya, just let me know the date and time and I will be there." "Thank you sweetheart" was my response. I always flirt, but I didn't mean to do it this time. Don't we all fight with temptations all day long???

Later that day, I felt so uneasy about going to Austin about his car. Now he probably thought he had me right where he wanted me, so I was no longer a challenge to him. I had to do something to ease the situation because I definitely didn't want him to think that I was trying to use him for his car. I was paranoid and pacing around my place like I was on crack. I needed to smoke a blunt. And I needed some good weed, not that fake stuff I heard people talking about! While blowing away my frustrations in the air through weed smoke, I started picturing how fly and cute I would look sitting on that car. I instantly jumped back into business mode: "Quality" is my motto and to whom much is given much is required. Everyone knows that scripture. I was selected as the Queen of the school, so why not represent it that way?

September 20, 2003 came and Vegas received an email from me about four weeks prior, explaining the date, time, and specifics. I also told him I had a gift for his volunteer efforts. When he arrived, he beat me to the punch. All I had was a cheap ass seventy-five dollar American Express gift card. Vegas showed up and showed out. He gave me yellow tulips, diamond studded earrings, a tennis bracelet, and two princess-cut diamond rings; one for the left and the other for the right. Don't hate ladies...I was Miss SSU and I had to present myself as an ambassador for the student body. *And he really liked ME*!!! The ball was definitely back in my court. Vegas even changed the rims and tires on his car. In his world, perception is everything. I must say he stepped up to the plate when he came with the jewelry. When he saw me, his beautiful dark brown eyes gave away how his heart was melting. Taylor, my home girl, hooked me up with a gorgeous vintage burnt orange fitted gown that hugged my boobs and bubble butt... She thought she was a stylist and I was her Ginny pig to try all of her new or whack ideas.

Tasha, the girl who did everybody's hair at school, was a great hair stylist. She hooked my hair all the way up. I didn't wear much makeup but just enough to enhance my eyes. When I saw the gifts, I was thinking, game on. But wait was I his territory now? Why did he buy me these gifts? Was this his way of buying me? I accepted the gifts because Ann always told me to be gracious and very accepting when someone gives. He reversed everything. I never received anything like that from Rod, Levin, or anyone but my father. My father always showered his baby girl with love.

"Austin why did you do all of this? This is too, too, too, much." "Koilya you are beautiful. I have been watching you since freshman year. This is what I wanted to tell you when you just happened to show up on my doorstep. You are one of smartest, flyest chics I know. You remind me of a Corporate Chic. And Chic without the K because you have style, girl swag and you are unique. There is something about you and I just can't see to shake you from my thoughts. I need someone like you in my life. Even if nothing ever happens between us, I am happy with just being your friend. These gifts are a drop in the bucket for me so please don't think I am a crazy ass dude with ill intentions."

I couldn't believe Vegas took the time to practice that sentence for about a month. Before he could say anymore, I butted in "Austin, I could never accept these items as gifts, but I can wear them in the parade today. When I said distinguished, I didn't mean Superstar. Hell, I just wanted to sit on a fly ass car for the parade! But I don't want to hurt your feelings by not accepting. So I'll accept them from you only for today. And where the hell did you learn to talk like that?!"

He looked at me and couldn't contain how giddy he was feeling on the inside.

I had to do or say something to break the ice.

He was acting super deep.

He grabbed me, saying at the same time, "Girl give me a hug. I am going to steal you away from Rod." Butterflies were in my stomach when he touched me. Needless to say that day was perfect. I felt like the queen of hearts and the world.

      Vegas thought he knew about my situation with Rod but he was all wrong. Dead wrong would be better. I dealt with Rod because he was a great friend. I was comfortable with Rod and didn't want to change a complacent situation. We connected on three of the four levels that I believe relationships should be based on. I really believe that true love exists between a male and a female when they connect spiritually, emotionally, mentally, and physically. I cannot be in any type of "ship" (that's partnership, friendship, or relationship) if the connection isn't with at least two of the four. Rod never gave me the title "girlfriend" and I accepted that and shouldn't have. I know a lot of females can agree here. I was Rod's "little" token chic for his Ivey league parents and their friends. Rod could have attended any school he wanted, but he came to an HBCU to prove a point. He told me he chose SSU because **Savannah State is the oldest public historically black university in Georgia.** He always used to jokingly say he felt like his great grandfather was black and he just knew he had African American blood running through his DNA. His parents were cool; but rich cool. He was an only child but his father taught him responsibility and the importance of hard work. It seemed like he was always trying to *show* them how we as humans were all created as one and the biggest difference was our gender. In our conversations about how he grew up in Cumming, Georgia, he would reminisce about some of the disturbing discussions about race with his mother's friends. He was very vocal about how much he disliked them because they felt entitled and privileged. He told me he would purposely start a conversation with them about race or being wealthy just so he could end it by saying we don't get to choose who our parents are, we are just born.

I would always tell him, I would have been the bitch to explain to him that we *do* get to choose. I read something many years ago that eluded to us being merely spirits and our spirits when chosen to come into this dimension (earth), choose the spirits that we wanted to transport us here. And because we chose that spirit, that spirit was responsible for being our guardians or parents. Rod would then follow up with, "Koilya whatever with your super deep shit...at the end of the day we are God's children and we all are equal. We should love one another and that's it.

It's that simple." And then I would respond by saying, "you sure have a funny way of showing your love Rod." Of course he would brush it off because he knew not being totally committed to me was a problem. His position on that matter was we were young and needed to live and experience life. We needed to explore. You know, the white people bullshit talk. But I accepted it because it was half way true. Although he didn't commit to me, I committed to him and for me, being committed meant that I wasn't a slut sleeping around and *exploring*.

Deep down I knew I would never fit in or be a part of such a conservative family. I am as authentic as they come. My skin is dark brown and I have to press my hair so that it is straight. I am opinionated, very intellectual and sarcastic. Rod loved it all but his obsession with proving that black was just a color to his parents, made me second guess him at times. He rebelled when it came to everything "white" when it came to his parents. Not to embarrass his family but to prove a point. My thoughts were always in the future and Rod was not in it. Even though that's where he placed me. Men are so smart that they are dumb. Rod trying to hold on to me until he was ready to settle down is what most men do. They don't realize, that's what causes a woman to stray. Once a woman's hope and faith starts to diminish, it is easy for another man to slip in; so, Vegas didn't have much stealing to do. But since he had that assumption, I would allow it to work to my advantage.

The love Rod and I had for each other, was reciprocal. Reciprocal meaning, he didn't bother to take it to the next level or figure out what I liked to do, so I responded by playing along. Our whole courtship was just something to do, although, our sexual chemistry was amazing. The white boy didn't lack in that area. When he ate my girl-girl it felt like he was softly kissing my lips…on my face. His tongue was so warm and he took his time, every time. That urban legend about black men being the only men with big dicks was so untrue. Rod had an elephant trunk hanging between his legs. That's how I learned to suck a mean dick. Most of our interactions were oral. We both mastered how to make each other cum without penetration. I was fine with it because Ann raised me like the white girls; no penetration. She told me mastering oral sex is the quickest way to get a man to marry you.

Although Rod had unconscious issues with being in an interracial relationship, he wanted to change who I was and what I liked. I didn't have a problem being open and trying new things but he always wanted to do what he wanted to do. I never went hiking, skiing or kayaking until I met him. (White people stuff that I didn't like!) But I did it. Rod never wanted to hang out with me at a Jazz club or Poetry/Spoken Word session. That is what I enjoyed. We didn't have long talks about life and trips to South Beach or St. Lucia. We connected physically, spiritually, and mentally. But emotionally we just could never get on the same page. He was nothing like Vegas or Levin. Levin was my first real college love.

Levin and I had so much fun, but through him is when I learned that a college, single guy is not really trying to fully commit to one female. My high school sweetheart moved to California and the distance was a huge barrier for two eighteen year olds. Our relationship ended my freshman year of college and I didn't date anyone while I was trying to figure out who I was and what I wanted. I was celibate for nine months and promised not to give away my power to anyone. Well, I met Levin in my sophomore year and he literally swept me off my feet. He was a charming pretty boy. After about six months of faking the funk with me, I saw his true colors and how much of a womanizer he really was. Once Levin became a Kappa he "to the left" my ass with the quickness. I was heart broken over that because I shared so much with him and he was the first guy that I allowed to get close to me after my break up with my high school sweetheart.

Most of my junior year, I was single and I loved the freedom of being single. Occasionally, I dated and one of my rules were, "Don't ask, don't tell." Not having to answer to anyone and stress about the things my girlfriends would constantly complain about, allowed me to focus on what I wanted for my life. The downside to that is being really lonely. Being single for a really long time is not the business and a vibrator didn't do the trick for me. I wanted someone to suck these breasts and grab this ass. I needed true penetration.

When I finally decided to be open about dating, I met Rod in one of my Journalism classes. This guy had a way with words. *Pleasant words are a honeycomb, sweet to the soul and healing to the bones.* Ann made me remember that scripture once she found out that I liked to write. Proverbs 16:24. I will never forget that verse. Rod was popular, handsome, sophisticated and the coolest white guy at the school. The fact that he was open to dating someone outside of his race is what made our relationship interesting and intriguing. He didn't see color but culturally he hadn't adjusted. I liked him just as he was…sometimes. When we were required to do presentations for class, Rod would out do everyone. The fact of the matter was that he was a good guy and I wanted the exact opposite. He won me over through words and his proposed goals for his life. I loved that he was business savvy. But the relationship was dull and boring. *Literally.* Guys need to understand that how you treat a woman is how she will treat you (in most cases). That's how Koilya Privil works. Show me you care, and I will show you I am down (Brandy sung it best).

Vegas, my new and exciting boo, started coming over, and I am going to be honest, I was sprung from day one. He was so confident in making me his one and only; it was scary. I felt sort of controlled. He never dealt with someone like me and I never dealt with a guy that truly understood what I needed. I guess because I approached him about his car, he felt that I was weak for material things. So he would buy cheap heart felt gifts. If I didn't get tulips, I was getting Groupon specials. Some guys know exactly what to do and how to manipulate a female. If a guy figures out what a female is all about and she doesn't know the answers for herself; that guy will define who and what she should be. Point. Blank. Period. Isn't the new cliché' "It is what it is..." Another important life lesson...

I was having a ball. Just living life freely and how I thought it should go. I was partying with Vegas and living a destructive life and didn't even realize what I was doing to myself. I kept up with my priorities, but after a while things started to take a toll because of the huge responsibility I had as an ambassador, working as an intern, and trying to juggle two guys. I lied to Rod about Vegas and told him that we were just friends and absolutely nothing was going on. He was livid when he found out that I was actually placing Vegas' car in the parade verses his Audi. But he knew Vegas had a classier car. I lied to Vegas about Rod being my boyfriend. I wanted to be in control of this relationship. I figured Rod never wanted to fully commit and Vegas just wanted to have a good time, so why not enjoy the roller coaster ride. Right? I stopped growing and maturing into a productive individual. At this point, college was so fun. But when it's time to face the real world and get the hell on, it's time. Being with Vegas was allowing me to hold on to what was comfortable and I didn't recognize I was actually delaying opportunities in my life.

Vegas was always respectful to me. He was fun, always on the grind, slick as a fox, and forever networking. While dating, he didn't know that I knew his mother was sick and died from breast & lung cancer. He was the sole beneficiary on her life insurance policy and his family won a settlement for a mal-practice class action suit against a hospital in some little country ass town in Georgia. He was Wealthy. Not Hood Rich. He had the kind of money where there was no need for credit cards or loans. Debt free is how we both were living. You know, if you saw something you wanted, it would absolutely not effect or have an impact on your bank account or credit score. Yeah…like that. But what I could never figure out was why he tried to make people think that he was robbing folks. Vegas wouldn't bust a grape! Or would he? He still was very mysterious. Because there were certain things that he just didn't let me in about.

I found out about the Trust Estate account that his grandfather set in place for him while doing some research at my internship. His information was linked to the Investment Firm through lawyers who did business with us. The wires made into his lawyers' accounts were the connection I had to see any and everything I wanted to see about his account. But I never wanted him to know that I knew this about him, because he would think that I was only with him for his money. And if I ever revealed that I knew that he was really a good boy that fell into some money that may change our whole relationship. He didn't know my family-life situation in the beginning and I preferred it stay that way.

Vegas' grandfather was a major influence in his life. He was a wise old man. I slowly learned that Vegas was gifted with words and expressing emotions because he was raised by an old soul. My major was in Business and my minor was in Journalism, so writing was always a passion. I also was always interested in guys who had a way with words. So Vegas learned everything he knew from an old, rusty pimp (his grandfather) and I was raised by my parents and older brother.

When I say that brotha laid it down…he did the damn thang when it came to satisfying me sexually. If I didn't fall in love with him, I would be his pimp. Every woman needs a taste of some good wood. Vegas and I connected physically and almost emotionally. But mostly physically. At that point, I was in love with the "D" and we did hit two of the four in order for us to be in some type of "ship." Our very first encounter was amazing and is an experience I will never forget. At this point, Vegas was the fourth guy I had ever been with sexually. Whenever I would spend the night at his house, I would play the good girl role. I held on to my power for about six weeks and I am surprised he understood. Probably because he was kicking it with a fast ass hoochie in the city. But this particular night, I knew it was going down. I wore my *Honeydue* teddy and came to bed fresh out of the shower. I got really comfortable and pretended like I wasn't listening to him on the phone with one of his stupid ass friends, talking about their next "business" deal. He immediately hung up with whoever he was talking to and gave me his un-divided attention. Of course I played like a manikin lying there like I was asleep and allowed him to kiss all over my body. The *Hanae Mori* that I was wearing was like kryptonite. It drew him in and he was eating my girl-girl like it was a plate of food. He was very gentle but the way he kissed and licked my clit was insane. As he was licking my clit, his right hand was caressing my left breast. It was as if he had done this a million times. As he caressed my left breast, he grabbed my right ass cheek. He gripped it and caressed and sucked and licked. I couldn't resist and had to return the favor. I pushed him off of me and demanded control. He had to know that I was a freak in the sheets. As I straddled him, I began to suck his dick like a true white girl. I sucked and caressed his balls like I was in a porno show. I felt him about to release, so I went straight to his chest and began to flicker my tongue across his nipples to keep him aroused. He was moaning and was ready to stick his penis in my tight, dripping wet sweetness. I stopped him and began giving him the deepest throat he ever experienced. As my saliva drained down his eight to nine inches, I grabbed his dick and placed it directly on top of my girl-girl. I rubbed it, back and forth making him want to at least stick the head in. But I wouldn't let him. I just rubbed my clit up against his hard dick while grabbing all of his manhood for about sixty seconds. We both were leaking uncontrollably. I finally told him that I trusted him with my life and pushed his penis in my vagina. As he kissed my breast, he stroked my pussy in and out; in and out. I loved to talk during sex, so I gave him the edge he needed to let go and fuck me like he really wanted to. I told him that I wanted to ride his dick and show him how real women did it. I climbed on top and began to grip his dick with my pussy. I threw it at him every time and couldn't stop. The blunt and Ciroc that I had before I got to his house was doing all the work for me. As I rode his dick like a cowgirl, he couldn't hold his cum much longer. So I made sure that I got mine before he came. And he never was allowed to bust all in me. He knew that he had to pull out. Once we were done, I got up and went straight to the bathroom because I had to clean myself. I didn't want to wake up with a fishy smelling girl-girl. I also made sure to pee so I wouldn't get a urinary track infection. I heard to many horror stories! When I returned to bed, the only thing Vegas could say was, "You are going to have my baby." I giggled and fell asleep.

Vegas and I had the best sex life. It was off the chain and I couldn't get enough. He turned me on with just a touch. Butterflies went through my body with just the thought of spending time with him. When we met up we were going to have sex at least two to three times that day. I never experienced an orgasm until I had sex with Vegas. He made sure that I got mine before he got his.

I began to fall hard for this guy, but I never felt like the only chic. I got a lot of his time, but not all of it. And I was ok with that. I didn't want Vegas to think I was falling for him so my "Reciprocal Theory" came in handy all the time. Not having direct access to me anytime he felt it convenient, is what I think, won him over. He was also very spontaneous. We were always going out of town for parties or just for a trip for two. So we weren't really seen around the city where we went to school. Of course Rod never suspected anything because he was doing what he wanted to do and remember, I didn't have the title so he couldn't "check" me about anything.

The following semester it was on and popping! During the week, I was committed to being an ambassador for the school and entertaining Rod. Rod thought I would be in Florida with my mom on weekends but that's when I would spend time with Vegas. I think he liked it that way and we got along great because we only saw each other two-three days a week. Even though I had insecurities about our "down low" relationship, I never talked about it with him.

The fact that I was dating two guys at the same time was exciting and didn't bother me at ALL. Guys do it religiously and I wasn't married. This is when I understood my brother's statement about why men lie. But I was falling for Vegas in the worst way and I was going to be starting the next chapter of my life once I graduated from college. I knew without a shadow of doubt that Rod and I were not going to be an item. I told myself that I was graduating in May of 2004 and if there wasn't going to be any ties between me and Mr. Money Bags; I was cool with it being what it was. But if we were going to be together, forever, like I doodled in my notebook a million times, then I needed a sign.

Graduation week was insane! I was ripping and running like a Corporate Chic. The week I was graduating from college is when I found out I was pregnant. I was lucky because I didn't have to walk around campus pregnant and ashamed. My shame came when I had to tell my mother. More shame would come when I finally built of enough courage to tell Rod and Vegas that they could potentially be the father. Ann would have normally been upset in a situation like this, but she was happy that she would have a grandchild; someone to spoil and someone to keep her company. She was very lonely since the tragedy happened in our family. When I told her, she was very supportive, but she gave me the third degree about living like a slut. She couldn't understand why I was dating two guys and sleeping with them both. She even tried to send me to counseling thinking that I dated both guys because each one represented some parts of my brother and my dad. I had to set her straight really quick because that was not the reason. I would forget to take my birth control pills for like a day or two and then try to play catch up. This method DOES NOT work! I repeat this method DOES NOT work! With all the wrong I was getting away with, you would think that I could at least remember to take a birth control pill. My goodness what a sign?! On top of that it was a damn shame that I didn't know who fathered my child. Ann always used to tell me, *"There is something about a closet that makes a skeleton restless."* My mess finally caught up with me.

Rod and I used protection every single time but I was thinking anything could happen in a situation like this and I wasn't going to take any chances. Vegas and I, on the other hand, were like two newlyweds. He trusted me and I trusted him. We never used protection. The sex was so good, finding a condom was the last thing on our minds when we hooked up. HIV wasn't really prevalent in society as much as it is now. In college, we weren't trying to get the curable STD's. Boy, has that changed. Women shouldn't trust men or men shouldn't trust women with their life. Knowing one another's status should be a topic of discussion at some point before having sex or making love. Point. Blank. Period.

Vegas was happy because he was the last of his friends to not have a baby momma. Rod was probably hoping that it wasn't his because the first thing that came out of his mouth was terminating the pregnancy. At the end of the day he knew he would have to marry me if he fathered the baby and Rod had commitment issues. His parents would have it no other way. But what's crazy is that, as time moved on, and my belly started growing, he started to fall in love with the idea of having a child. Or was guilt starting to kick in? My theory was he wanted a reason to stay in contact with me because he probably felt guilt about never fully committing. I know Rod loved me but he never learned how to balance our relationship. In the back of his mind he always felt like he would have to explain to people why he was dating a black girl. He knew people didn't know right off the bat by just seeing me that I was educated and intelligent. When we were together the stares and remarks would get to him. My dad always told me that *He, who angers you, controls you* and because I understood that, I became a pro at ignoring folks. I didn't allow people to upset me. Especially about, who, I decided to date; that was none of their business.

Although, I was hesitant about telling them both; I was forced to deal with the reality of my situation and I had to tell Rod the truth about me and Vegas and Vegas the truth about Rod and I. Vegas knew that I was Rod's "so-called girlfriend" so he knew that there could be a possibility of him not being the father. Once Vegas and I started to get really close, I told him Rod and I weren't having sex and he actually believed me. Vegas took the news way too smooth though. When I told Rod that I needed to have a blood test once the baby was born, he instantly knew that Vegas was in the equation. One thing about a lie is that you have to keep telling them in order not to get caught. I was tired of lying. Once I told both guys, I knew I would lose their loyalty. But I had to tell them both the truth so that I could sleep at night.

From the day I decided to tell Vegas the truth, I lost my true love. He never really trusted me even though he said he did. It didn't matter that he never confessed or I didn't catch him with another chic, but I knew I didn't have his whole heart. In his mind, I was not the same girl that he fell in love with on the day I stood at his door steps with my planner and bright smile. I saw the difference in some of his actions. Rod moved to Miami after graduating.

I became a full time employee with the Investment Firm and transferred to their headquarters in Atlanta. Rod would travel to Atlanta once a month to attend doctor appointments with me. He always said that it was the least he could do. But Rod was messing around with someone in Atlanta. He thought I didn't know, but I did and could care less. Vegas stayed in Savannah and finished up school, but best believe every other weekend he was in Atlanta.

I was doing a great job at work and I hid my pregnancy until I was about six months. That was a shame too, but I wanted to learn as much as I could before the baby was born. With a maternity leave of about eight weeks, I was putting in work and doing a great job along the way. I wanted to be recognized as a great employee so management could see how much of an asset I was to the company. I didn't need any stories about how great of an employee I was, but wasn't an asset to the company once I returned from my leave. So I ensured that my clients only dealt with me. My clients received quality service and a whole lot of perks. I gave away free trips, spa days, and football game tickets. I had loyal clients who would sever their relationship with the Investment Firm if they were unable to have me as their Manager. That was always important to me.

After ten long antagonizing months, my baby was born on my brother's birthday. I knew this baby was going to be special. Ann held and rocked my baby like she was never going to see him again. The paternity test was done immediately. Both Rod and Vegas were at the hospital and there was no drama. We all were filled with guilt and this baby was our reason. The doctor gave me the news first and then I had to deliver the news to them. From the time I knew Vegas, this was the first thing he didn't bet on.

When I think of U, I think of lust.
Tricks,
Mr. Lova
is what I saw when U came into my presence.
But challenges are my forte.
When I first saw U (on a friendly level)
U stopped me

dead N my tracks!
For once N forever my flesh took over my mind & convinced my
heart 2 give U & us a try.
U know, C what U were talking about.
if U could B that guy,
if U shared the same morals,
if U could be my man, my boo on my Level, talk 2 U about
Me & U & Us.
Combine 2 worlds that N contrast maybe somewhat opposite, but
not really.
All at once I was forced 2 think about
My Vision,
which is seeing beyond the present.
My deepest desire
is 2 love GOD with my all & be happy; forget money & a degree!
My passion
is 2 become 1 with a man & submit with a consummation.
Handling my "cat" is not difficult,
but
Handling my mind & my heart is more than a task.
It is what HE is supposed 2 do 4 Me & Us.
Mr. Fresh! I can Dress! I love being me....I won't change.
U R your own idol and U have the potential 2 B A Good man.

But U have 2 get over U.

TNG

42

How you exit one thing determines how you enter another.
~**Mountain Wings**

Introducing Miss Koilya Privil

My dad was the only person that sacrificed for me and my brother. He gave us what we needed and wanted. But when my brother was killed in Iraq by a suicidal bomber, my father died shortly after from a broken heart. I was fifteen years old ascending into my junior year of high school. Ever since then it's been me and Ann. Ann is my mom and she is my best friend in the whole world. Now that I am older, I call her by her first name. It's something we both decided. This is the only way she doesn't treat me like a child, when I am telling her something that she may not want to hear, but has to listen to because I need her advice. We have a beautiful relationship; we can talk to each other about anything. I am not bias when it comes to her. If she is wrong, she is wrong. If I am wrong about certain things that she advises me of, I am wrong. I've experienced almost all of what she went through as a young woman and more because I am so out-going and curious. So I think that is what brings the balance. Plus she lives vicariously through my many life events.

It took my mother a very long time to get over the death of my brother and my dad. Eventually, I got over it, but my mom still grieved through my entire first year of college. And we came up with a ritual to call each other once a day to say a prayer my dad taught her. I came home every weekend to make sure she was ok. This was extremely hard for her. To bury a son and a spouse within six months was painful for us both. Once I understood that death is a reality that everyone some point or another has to face, that alone helped but it didn't really cure me. Some people have to deal with death earlier in life. I eventually became okay and at peace with loving them both from a distant. I think this is when I started smoking weed heavily.

I felt like the Imitation of Life was just a movie and didn't know people could actually die from having a broken heart until it happened to my father. He died from heart failure six months after he saw Kevin's picture on the news as one of the fallen soldiers. Kevin was like my father's mini-protégé. My daddy was a Seminole Indian and was very well off. I remember my father grooming Kevin into the man that he became. My father told Kevin that he needed to be wise because he was going to leave him a great inheritance. My father gave him all sorts of tests and taught him rituals that he would one day pass down to his children. Legacy was significant to us. My family owned acres and acres of land in Florida although we didn't live on a reservation. Everything my father taught Kevin, Kevin taught me. He taught me the value of money and the importance of saving money. At first I didn't listen, but learned quickly that money is the easiest way to attract fake people. Needless to say, I loved my father and my brother so much. They both were always there for us and my father loved my mother unconditionally. Ann was from a small town in South Carolina. She met my dad while attending Florida State. She really wasn't with all that Native American stuff and meant that she was going to Americanize her children. We had my mother's last name because she had us both before my father married her. She told him that was his punishment. It shouldn't have taken him seven years to marry her. But she respected my father and loved him to death. Literally.

Kevin was a great big brother. We would fight all the time because he was so over-protective; but what big brother doesn't look out for his little sister? We covered for each other; told each other everything, and I am the reason he would date the flyest chics at school. He is the person that showed me how to roll my own blunt. I wrote all his papers for his allowance and we had a bond that I will always cherish forever in my memories. My brother only lived to see nineteen. We all know that's not long at all. My father enlisted him in the army telling him that he needed more discipline after he found a pound of weed in his room. Father was outraged that day! He just knew my brother had the intention of distributing it. When Kevin told me about it, I told him to bury that mess outside because he knew that daddy was an old nosey snoop. But Kevin really was holding it for one of his friends. Daddy didn't believe him and enlisted him. I guess that's why he took it so hard.

I truly believe that Kevin served his purpose. The way I understand this life thing is we live until our purpose is served and once it is, we transition to the other side of life. I believe that about Kevin but not with my father. I think he prematurely ended his life. He became severely depressed. There was nothing no one could say or do to bring him back. I would hear him telling God that he should have taken his life and not Kevin's. He would say that Kevin was still a little boy and that he lived his life. Ann tried to make sense of the whole thing by telling him that Jesus died and that God lost his only son for us, so there was a bigger purpose in Kevin's death. But my father just believed that he was being taught a lesson for his past transgressions.

I ended up inheriting double because my brother signed everything over to me when he enlisted. Kevin was smart enough to make sure that there was a clause in his will that stated I couldn't access it until I was thirty. My father also had a will in place and the $110.5 million that he made in working his own business is what really made me a Wealthy Chic. It's a big difference in being wealthy and becoming rich. "Rich money" will run out, if it is not governed properly. I wouldn't become a wealthy chic until I was in my mid thirties. My father must have told my brother how he had his will arranged because Kevin's will was exactly the same. My inheritance is split into increments. I receive small fixed amounts at 18, 21, and 25 and then thirty percent of the entire inheritance at 30; thirty percent at 40 and the last amount at 50. I guess he set it up that way because he knew that having too much money at one time would burn my pockets. I was forced to learn the value of money. My dad built an empire off of his land and his travel business.

Ann had everything on lock. She was not a lighthearted spender. She was the complete opposite of my father. She only made sure she got what she needed and definitely ensured I received what I needed. Not wanted. No more than that. But that's what sort of helped me stay grounded. She believed that everything someone needs, they will always have with or without money. I must admit that sometimes I could spend too much, but I didn't do it all the time. I never knew what we were worth until I started working at USA Investment Firm. I had access to all sorts of computer programs and I was a snoop...

I was sent off to college with $25,000 in my checking account, $50,000 in my Money Market Savings, and an additional $150,000 in a CD that I could not touch. After I ran through $20,000 in the first year (and this was not tuition), I was forced to find out about Suze Orman. The money, at first, was how I coped. But Ann locked all of my money down. Once I found out who Suze Orman was and what she represented {Money and Women}, I started to take all the advice she had to offer. Ann was tired of me spending money frivolously and reminded me of this every time I went to the ATM. She told me I had to maintain money while it grew because anything could happen.

*God uses finances to teach us to trust him and for many people money is the greatest test of all. God watches how we use money to test how trustworthy we are. Life is a TEST and TRUST and the more God gives you, the more responsible he expects you to be! ~**Anonymous***

Native American Prayer for the Grieving
Unknown

I give you this one thought to keep-I am with you still, I do not sleep.
I am a thousand winds that blow, I am the diamond glints on snow, I am the sunlight on ripened grain, I am the gentle autumn rain.
When you awaken in the morning's hush, I am the swift uplifting rush of quiet birds in circled flight.
I am the soft stars that shine at night.
Do not think of me as gone-I am with you still in each new dawn.

Speak 2 my Heart: My Conversation with God

U remember the phony friends?
Gold diggas lookin 2 ride N A Benz
& the guy that would make u sin...
Remember the keys 2 the jeep
trips 2 South Beach, living a fantasy just cause u don't know or
have a relationship with ME....

BUT I like my life....

And HE said IT'S NOT YOUR Life.
YOU ARE DESTINED TO FULFILL YOUR PURPOSE.

Determination = Persistence
Giving your all in everything you do,
Builds your Character
Keeps you Strong
Can't go Wrong
Mistakes have been made
but your debts have been paid.
I have learned a lot from error in my ways...
Life lessons are critical.
If you miss class, you won't pass
Adversity is your strength.
U asked me to speak to you heart...well I just did.

TNG

A friend knows you <u>very well</u> and still likes you.

–Dr. A.R.Bernard

Chapter 2:
Friendship

Friendship is built on a foundation of mutual interests and common goals using the tools of loyalty, acceptances, and selfless deeds. ~**Anonymous**

*I don't care. I didn't care. And I won't care. ~**Kali***

March 3, 2005

Alexander, Kali is starting this conversation with the message:
Good morning!!!

Liegel, Karla has been added to the instant message conversation:

Alexander, Kali
How was y'all's weekend?

Liegel, Karla
Boring

Liegel, Karla has left the instant message conversation.

Privil, Koilya
Good Morning!
My weekend was full alright
Both families were in town for the
dedication
And we had a good time
What did u do?

Alexander, Kali
Not much
L.A is home with Cole
I went out with this guy
He seemed cool
But they all seem cool in the beginning…

51

Privil, Koilya
In the beginning...But give it a chance
Just don't be too fast...hey...that rhymes...lol

Alexander, Kali
I'm not

Privil, Koilya
But on the real these days you have to take
things slow because eventually u want
someone to "BE With"

Alexander, Kali
You make me smile

You are right

He's crazy though

He's already talking about being in a

relationship

U know I DRIVE THEM CRAZY!!!

**Leigel, Karla has been added to the instant message
conversation.**

Karla and Kali were my co-workers. We were in the office or
working more than we were home. We developed a friendship
through chatting on Instant Message. Kali worked in Trust/Estate
Account Management with the Interns. But Karla and I were in
Client Management & Internal Fraud.

The fraud that is happening within Investment/Corporate companies is ridiculous! We decreased fraud and maintained the companies' clientele by protecting the company and the customers' money. It's funny that the majority of fraud committed in most companies, are done by their employees or ex-employees. Statistics prove that employee theft will continue to cost businesses about $40 billion (yes with a B) annually. It is getting harder and harder in the corporate world to protect an organization's information, as well as their, physical and intellectual property. A corporation's property, personnel, and intellectual assets must be protected. Failure to ensure this will interrupt any success a company has ever experienced. So this is where we came in the picture.

We all met through an internship/pilot department. We assisted in saving the company over sixty-four million dollars and because we were a part of the initial pilot, we were all hired permanently. The job was very stressful and things were just getting out of control within the department. The Executives that ran the department sucked worse than a straw. There wasn't any room for growth and employee morale was extremely low. If you were not a part of the click KA&SC/"Kissing Ass and Smoking Cigarettes" getting promoted should have not crossed your mind. Education didn't matter because the people who were in charge of the department only had experience. *No education.* So imagine what it felt like being on a sinking boat and the captain of the boat had no direction and could never be a leader.

Kali decided to leave the department but went back to help the interns. I always say change is good. Because it keeps a person adapting to life and it's many waves. But going backwards is always going backwards.

Alexander, Kali
```
There aren't any good jobs posted
```

Liegel, Karla
```
Nope
```

Alexander, Kali
```
What is a girl to do?
```

Privil, Koilya
```
Be patient
```

Alexander, Kali
```
I can't take it
I hate this job
```

But she went back to the job. She said the same exact words six months prior!

Alexander, Kali
```
I'm about to apply for a Premier Client
Manager position and see what happens
It would be helpful if I could get Series 6
and 7 licenses
```

Privil, Koilya
Me 2 but u have to understand that in life
you have to do what you got to do to
live…and right now this is our
livelihood…this is how the bills are
paid…until we can get into a better
situation, we have to be happy where we are
in our lives now in order to advance to the
next step or journey in our life.

Alexander, Kali
I don't believe that. Because I'm not happy
And this will not ever make me happy
I have to find my happiness…I can't sit and
wait for it to find me
At least that is the way that I think. It
might not be right. But it is my philosophy

Privil, Koilya
You will never get anything in life without
being happy with where God has u. . .It's
called being content Kali.

Alexander, Kali
I am not happy with my job, but I am happy
that God wakes me up every morning

Privil, Koilya
To come to work and pay my bills

Alexander, Kali
Right
Oh yes…definitely…don't get me wrong…I am
blessed to have a job, but I don't like what I
do

Privil, Koilya
U have to understand that in order for u to
get anything worth having you r going to

have to work for it, go through some trial
and tribulations and then when you get what
u deserve, you will realize why it is so
important that the tough times come.
Life isn't easy honey
Everyday you are tested and you will not
move to the next place in your life until
you pass the tests that God has for you to
become a better person.
That's the only way
You have so many ideas and then the next
day you don't want to do it
You need to figure out your purpose…

Kali was all over the place. I hated having certain conversations with her. One day she told me she wanted to be a bartender. Because I support my friends and their choices, I went out and bought a "How to"…Bartending book. That book is still sitting on my night stand dusty as hell. The next week she wanted to become a barber and open up a barber shop. What the hell?! I never knew where the ideas came from or why they popped up in her brain. She was always looking for different things to do. And she had absolutely no direction in where she wanted her life to go.

The only thing she was sure about was her daughter L.A. Kali was a single mom making really good money but didn't manage it properly. She always cried about not having help. L.A.'s dad wasn't a good fit for Kali so they didn't really get along. He was in the Navy. Cole was some high ranked uppity sailor with an attitude. He lived in California and Kali lived in Atlanta. She preferred it stay that way. Whenever Cole wanted to see L.A., Kali never held his daughter away from him. For the most part, they got along for the kid. But they couldn't agree on anything else. Kali was care free, and drama free; I will give her that. She didn't deal with the drama. She always tried to chomp people off by being sarcastic or slick at the mouth but when she tried that shit with me or Karla we always knew how to put her back in her place.

Alexander, Kali
```
That is just me (Kali)
I operate like that
Always have
```

Privil, Koilya
```
Once you figure out your purpose and what
you know without a shadow of a doubt you
are supposed to be doing, then things will
begin to become a little easier for you.
U can have your way of doing things-that's
cool- we all do but you need to figure out
what u really want to do with your
life…with no direction you will never know
where u r going
```

Liegel, Karla
```
PREACH
```

Anytime Karla thought Kali and I were bumping heads or having a disagreement she always butted in to ease our egos. Get the hell out of here Kali with that dumb bull shit is what I really wanted to tell her. Bouncing from one job to another was crazy to me but she lived by Colin Powell's statement: *You can't make someone else's choices so you shouldn't let someone else make yours.* So I couldn't hate or push my views on her. I wasn't perfect. Plus, we both thought we were right and we weren't backing down from our opinions. I wasn't being sold on what she had to say and she wasn't trying to hear what I was saying.

Liegel, Karla
Amen
I FEEL U

Alexander, Kali
You crazy ☺
All late

Liegel, Karla
SHUT UP
Better late than never

Alexander, Kali
I guess
☺

Liegel, Karla
LOL ☺

Alexander, Kali
I found a new spot to hang out at
Off of Moreland
A sports bar called Driftwood
They don't card to get in

Liegel, Karla
I CALLED U THIS WEEKEND!
WAS IT NICE?

Alexander, Kali
```
Yeah
It was packed
And Ghetto
But it was white and black people
It was funny
```

Liegel, Karla
```
U R SO LAME
I wanted to go…
```

Alexander, Kali
```
I was on a date
Be happy for me ☺
```

Liegel, Karla
```
O ok
I'm happy and hating ☺
```

Alexander, Kali
```
LOL…I understand
```

Liegel, Karla
```
I need a date
```

Karla was a couple of years younger than Kali and I. But she was on the top of her game. She had a son, owned a home, and was making $52,000 annually at twenty-one. She didn't go to college and through networking and just having a beautiful personality she landed a great paying job. But she was single. Leland, her son's dad, was locked up and convicted of Embezzlement & Grand Larceny. Word is he embezzled over $5.6 million into a Grand Cayman Island account. He also was committing bank fraud which is a federal & state offense. Because he got greedy; he got caught. But the messed up part about all this money he supposedly had, was that he didn't give Karla any. People need to realize; a belly full is a belly full. After going through hell and back with her child's father, Karla was forever looking for love and in all the wrong places.

Liegel, Karla
Was it with the mover?

Alexander, Kali
Yeah
Girl he is crazy
He's already talking about moving together!
But overall he's cool

Liegel, Karla
Lol ☺
That's good
We'll c what happens
Don't run him away
Lol ☺

Alexander, Kali
Whatever
I don't run them away…I gets rid of them…
take out the trash…if you know what I mean

Liegel, Karla
Lol ☺
I feel u

Alexander, Kali
Well what are you doing this week?

Liegel, Karla
I don't know

Privil, Koilya
Ok I am back...I had a little phone meeting
and then went to lunch
What's up with this new club/hang-out spot?

Alexander, Kali
I found a new beauty shop
It is nice

You see how she just jumped subjects! She was notorious for changing the subject and I hated it! But because I knew the type of person she was, I dealt with it for the most part.

Privil, Koilya
Who, where, and cost

Alexander, Kali
Flat shoals past South Dekalb Mall
Same
Called Ricks Cuts and Styles

Privil, Koilya
A guy does the hair?

Alexander, Kali
They have about ten beauticians and five
barbers
No

Privil, Koilya
Oohhh

Alexander, Kali
Rick just owns it

Privil, Koilya
Who does your hair?

Alexander, Kali
Really nice and clean
A girl named Toccarra
Sabrina would make some money if she worked
there
Toccarra has my hair super straight and I
don't have a perm!
Well I haven't had one since November

Privil, Koilya
That's what's up
I hope she works out
I feel so loyal to Sabrina
Until she does me wrong I may have to stick
with her
But as soon as she slips I know where I can
come to get my hair done

Sabrina was our hair stylist. She was really good at doing hair but
she had a nasty, *diva* attitude. I think Sabrina was misunderstood.
Kali introduced me to her. She used to do all of Kali's colors.
Sabrina was a pro at weave and color. So I started going to her
while I was pregnant and have been going ever since. Kali
stopped going to Sabrina because she said Sabrina had an attitude
problem. Karla went to her for a while too, but she stopped going
because of Sabrina's attitude. I didn't see it or was probably blind
toward it. Because the sista could hook you all the way up! Or

maybe she was extra nice to me because I referred about five people to her, either way, I was going to be loyal to Sabrina.

Alexander, Kali
```
I'm sure it's plenty of places…I just
finally tried somewhere else
But I am pleased
```

Privil, Koilya
```
That's good
So what's up with this mover? And do I come
off as thinking that I know everything,
because I don't want to seem like a momma
```

I felt sort of bad about jumping all over Kali…

Alexander, Kali
```
You are a momma
```

Privil, Koilya
```
I just learn through my life and want to
tell you if I can help
```

Alexander, Kali
```
Mama!
```

Privil, Koilya
```
I know but not yours
```

Liegel, Karla
```
Lol ☺
Ya'll a mess
```

Privil, Koilya
```
I just don't want to come off like a know
it all
```

That's all
KARLA!

Liegel, Karla
Lol ☺
Yeah, yeah, yeah
Lol ☺

Alexander, Kali
Girl I ain't trippen…I take the advice I
want…and the rest…I listen…but might not
apply. I know that nobody is perfect that
is why it is hard for me to take anyone's
advice. I'm hard headed

Leigel, Karla
Yes! Very!
Lol ☺

Alexander, Kali
Whatever
But that is what makes me-me!
BUT NE WAYS
The mover guy is CRAZY KOILYA!
He seems nice but he has stalker
capabilities!!! Just playing
He's cool though
He has his own business

Liegel, Karla
$$$$$$$$$$$

Privil, Koilya
Money, money, money ☺

We didn't know everybody who said they had a business didn't
have money…..(lol ☺)

Privil, Koilya
I hope it works out. . . I just don't want
my friends to be like don't tell Koilya she
is going to preach. . .lol ☺
Like Karla said
But NE way…
That's my spiel
So you went to an all white club?
Lol ☺
By the way have ya'll heard of Blue Light?

Alexander, Kali
No it was not a white people club

Privil, Koilya
Lol ☺
Just playing
Goodness

Alexander, Kali
It was a black club, but white people was
there…It was crazy

Privil, Koilya
We need to go
This weekend since Joshua is gone

Alexander, Kali
L.A. is back

Privil, Koilya
I didn't know she left
I should have called you back Saturday

Liegel, Karla
Koilya shut up
I did not mean it like that
Kinsasha JR
LOL ☺

rivil, Koilya
```
Queen!
Please don't call me that
LOL ☺
```

Kinsasha, aka Queen, was one of the females who interned with us. Karla and Queen came from the same department. So they were really good friends when we met them. Queen was a hopeless case though. She would come to work dressed homely and she hated her life and the situation she was in but she did nothing to make her situation better. She was always complaining about something. She was married to a guy name Randy for five years. Randy was a dope boy and he was in the game at a point of no return. Queen was pushing a Range Rover with twenty-four inch rims. Her wedding ring sparkled like a disco ball. She had several rings, bracelets, a Rolex, and hand bags. (This woman had every designer bag you could name or think of.) The sad part about having designer bags, clothes, and jewelry is that she didn't know how to rock her gear. Her husband cheated on her several times with local strippers. He even had outside kids but she refused to leave because she had become accustomed to the life style. It would only be a matter of time before he suffered the consequences of his actions. Everyday Queen came to work she had a story about Randy. And all of the stories resulted in Queen crying or someone consoling her. And Queen was defensive as all get out and tried to justify all of her actions.

Privil, Koilya
```
I am not that pathetic
Lol ☺
Not Queen
```

Liegel, Karla
```
WELL STOP BEING SO DEFENSIVE
```

Privil, Koilya
```
Ok
```

Liegel, Karla
```
I didn't know that Sharise went to SC with
Keith???!!!
```

And we were good for gossiping! Sharise was an old friend of mine. In my sophomore year, we worked at *The Stagg Shoppe*, which was an elite, urban clothing store that sold Hip Hop gear in Savannah, GA. Sharise used to be married to this lame, no-working type of brotha. She had a little girl by him and her mother forced her to get married. Well, after three years of being married and being separated numerous amounts of times, Sharise finally called it quits with Adrian. Sharise was the type of person that would take any hand-outs. She was always complacent with where she was in her life. I helped her get a job in the department Karla and I worked. Her mother paid her bills, took control of her paycheck, told her to divorce her husband, and she did it. Her mother was a retired woman that had an opinion about everything and everybody. And because Sharise's mom was helping her with everything, she felt obligated to do whatever her mom said. So

Sharise and I came into the Internship together. Karla and Kinsasha came in together and Kali was a loner.

Sharise has two kids, MaKayla and Peter, with her ex-husband. Karla and Sharise started to get really close and my friendship with Sharise was drifting. Mostly because her ex-husband made her believe that I was interested in him. When he found out that Sharise was leaving him and he would have to be responsible (get a job, pay bills + pay child support), he was pulling all kinds of tricks out of his bag to keep Sharise. One of the lies or manipulative things he did was make her believe that I was interested in him. And she actually believed it! I was hurt and disappointed that a friend, whom I trusted, didn't trust me. I never did anything to make her feel like I would want her SORRY-ASS, NO MONEY having ex-husband! I couldn't believe that she thought I would do that! I could play the heck out of a male or his friend, but a female who is my friend, I couldn't do it. Keith is a co-worker who came into the department after us and Sharise was desperate and interested.

Privil, Koilya
No!!!
!!
She has never told me about him

Liegel, Karla
Oops
Lol ☺

Privil, Koilya
The only thing she said once was that he
came over to see MaKayla & Peter

Liegel, Karla
I didn't know it was a secret
She just told me this today

Privil, Koilya
Well because I am not supposed to know
anything I played it like he was just a co-
worker coming to visit the baby

Liegel, Karla
And I think it was by accident that she
told me about this
She was talking about how Peter is so good
on road trips...

Privil, Koilya
I hope it works out
mmmmmmmmmmmmmmmmmmmmmmmmmmmmmmmmmmmmmmmmmmmmmmmmmmm

Liegel, Karla
And I was like did u have to stop more than
once

Privil, Koilya
She gets the long
mmmmmmmmmmmmmmmmmmmmmmmmmmmmmmmmmmmmmmmmmmmmmmmmmmm

Liegel, Karla
And she was like naw I rode with Keith

Privil, Koilya
What!

Liegel, Karla
I was like whhhhhhhhhhhhhhhhhat

Lol ☺

Privil, Koilya
U know her momma gave her that E-CLASS
Liegel, Karla
I hope my face didn't show what I was
thinking...

Privil, Koilya
Well she has to pay for it

Liegel, Karla
Because I got a bad habit of that

Karla and Sharise sat in the same area. I was upstairs and they
were downstairs. And we were literally talking about her in her
face.

Privil, Koilya
He may do right by her
And I have that same problem too
What I am thinking shows

Liegel, Karla
Yea I know

Privil, Koilya
That's a mess
But he may really like her

Liegel, Karla
Yea that's y I'm not hating

When Keith first came into the department, he tried to hook up
with Karla and Sharise. Karla was too smart for Keith and his

70

games, but Sharise took the bait. She was hurt about the circumstances and the cards she was left to deal with and for some strange reason she always thought that her friends wanted the man she was dealing with. One by one she began to cut people out of her life because of insecurity issues. Back to Keith…

Liegel, Karla
```
He was going to visit his daughter so they
rode together
That's what Sharise says
Maybe he went up there to meet the fam…Lol
☺
```

Privil, Koilya
```
Not this early
Her momma doesn't play that
```

Liegel, Karla
```
We don't know how long this has been going
on
```

Privil, Koilya
```
She isn't even divorced yet
```

Liegel, Karla
```
True
```

Privil, Koilya
```
If it's a secret then there is something to
hide
```

Liegel, Karla
```
Yep
```

Privil, Koilya
Did she tell you about the car her momma
let her get?

Liegel, Karla
Yep
That's why she is trying to sell hers

Privil, Koilya
Right...She's selling her car to her sisters'
son

Alexander, Kali
Ya'll crazy
Girl...I need to see if her car is parked at
his house
Doesn't Keith live around the corner from
me?
How has Kinsasha been?

Privil, Koilya
Ask Karla, her co-signer

Alexander, Kali
KARLA??? Ya'll silly, I wish I still worked
with ya'll
Privil, Koilya
Me 2
We miss u

Alexander, Kali
I know...I really want to get on a 9-6pm
shift over there
If they ever bring that back let me know

Privil, Koilya
I won't...I told u not to move backward

I was not about to tell her to come back to the department she just left six months prior. Kali was never going to get anywhere in her life flip flopping between the same two jobs.

Privil, Koilya
And u think that u hate Trust Management
with the Interns…

Alexander, Kali
I would only come back for school purposes

Privil, Koilya
Girl u will despise Investments & Fraud

Alexander, Kali
I know girl

Privil, Koilya
We can't even use our cell phones on the
floor!

Employees were compromising clients' information and selling their personal information. Identity Theft was on the rise and it was bananas trying to follow the money to ensure it wasn't fraud. We lost an enormous amount of capital due to internal theft; it was crazy. Certain scams and tricks that only employees knew about were being done consistently. All of the Analyst & Managers knew that employees were making money by selling the information but the Execs didn't have a clue. So to reduce the possibility of internal theft, cell phones weren't permitted nor were back packs. All papers were to be shredded daily. Nothing came in the building and nothing left the building. And if you brought a lunch bag, the toy cops would make you late. They searched like the airport security guards!

Privil, Koilya
```
We have to go out where the elevators are
to use the phone
There is to too much micro-managing &
security act like we are terrorist!
```

Liegel, Karla
```
Lol ☺
And I am not a co-signer Koilya ☺
```

Privil, Koilya
```
Lol...☺
Yes 4 Queen U R
```

Liegel, Karla
```
No I'm not
```

Privil, Koilya
```
U take up 4 her 2 much
Old Miserable bitch
```

Liegel, Karla
```
I do that with everybody
```

Privil, Koilya
```
No...that's your pearl
```

Liegel, Karla
```
I just know she has some psychological
issues
So I'm more understanding ☺
```

Karla made excuses for everybody instead of allowing people to be responsible for their actions. Being unusually nice always gets you burned. I am a no-non-sense type person: Point Blank. Period.

Privil, Koilya
That's what she uses so people can feel
sorry for her when she acts the way she
does
Kali…right or wrong?

Liegel, Karla
U have to get more background info
This is not a new issue

Privil, Koilya
U know she told me all her business
All
Of
It
We used to sit right by each other!
There is no reason for a 35 year old woman
to act like a puppy

Liegel, Karla
I think she just needs to get professional
help and get away from that evil family of
hers

Privil, Koilya
Because it would have been different if she
didn't have it in her to do better…she
knows what to do to get out of the
situation she is in

Liegel, Karla
It takes a lot more for some people to get

over the tragic things that occur in their
life

Privil, Koilya
Yes her family has a lot to do with it but
she is a huge contributor
She thinks she ain't nothing without a
Gucci purse
She is VERY materialistic

Liegel, Karla
U gotta think though its how u r raised

I was raised around a lot of money but I wasn't a fool and plus
Vegas got all hemmed up in a crazy situation and there was a lien
on all of our money and assets. He possibly could do a bid (go to
jail) for Conspiracy if he lost the trial. My baby and I were
struggling! I didn't want Ann to know what was going on
because she already went through enough with our family
tragedy and me doing whoe-ish things like not knowing who my
baby daddy was. So I did hide this particular situation from her. I
wasn't straight like my college days, but I never fell off on
looking good. And neither did my little boy. I never spent the
type of money Queen spent. She lived her life like a celebrity on
drugs! She never was fly; but she had all the potential to be.

Privil, Koilya
And if you look better than her than she
doesn't speak

Liegel, Karla
It's a learned behavior

Privil, Koilya
...I am rolling my eyes!

Liegel, Karla
And it's hard to break that

Privil, Koilya
She's too insecure
But y would I get mad at you because u take
care of yourself?
That's not psychological, that's jealousy

Liegel, Karla
?... I'm clueless

Privil, Koilya
It's two totally different things...
When Queen see a female looking cute or
something, she acts like she can't speak.
She has done it to me several times and I
would let it roll off my back. But u only
have so many times to chomp me off

Liegel, Karla
U know I'm not the one to notice stuff like
that because that would never bother me

Privil, Karla
The last time I spoke to her, she was all
cool (this was on IM) but when I came up
there she through major shade...and I am not
with that BS

Liegel, Karla
Or I'm just very non-caring

Privil, Koilya
She probably doesn't do it to u
But u can feel negative energy
And I'd rather not be around that

Liegel, Karla
That's what I'm saying I can't vouch for
that type of behavior

Privil, Koilya
Right
Yeah she was really rude when I came up
there
Any other time she is joking and laughing
But the last couple of times I went up
there to speak to some of the other co-
workers she threw shade like Bitch don't
speak to me

Liegel, Karla
Lol ☺ Girl U R CRAZY

Privil, Koilya
Lol ☺
U think I am playing
I can tell when a girl is acting shady

Liegel, Karla
Koilya you say that about everybody

Privil, Karla
I do?

Liegel, Karla
aaahhhh…Yes
Lol ☺

Privil, Koilya
I guess I got a lot of haters

Liegel, Karla
Lol ☺

Privil, Koilya
People don't usually like me though
I've dealt with that my whole life

Liegel, Karla
That's y u r always defensive

Privil, Koilya
The only reason y ya'll are friends with me
is because I was pregnant when u really got
to know me. Ya'll didn't see me as a stuck
up chic. I wasn't intimidating all fat and
pregnant.

Liegel, Karla
Girl shut up

Privil, Koilya
That's probably why I am so defensive
Lol ☺
4real
When I first met you and Queen
Queen never really spoke to me
She would speak to Sharise

Alexander, Kali
Stop typing you guys

Privil, Koilya
I remember

Liegel, Karla

And no it wasn't because u were pregnant
that we became your friend. Because
pregnant people r the most difficult
So y be friends for just that reason
U r sweet (sometimes) and nice (sometimes)
Lol ☺

Privil, Koilya

Lol ☺

Liegel, Karla

And when we first got into the pilot
program; u and Sharise used to work
together and so did me and Queen so we had
our little click thing going
But like in all class situations u learn
more about the people u around and u
befriend those who u want in your circle
So don't put that "just because I was
pregnant" mess on me missy ☺

Privil, Koilya

Lol ☺

Liegel, Karla

Because u r not pregnant anymore

Privil, Koilya

People perceive me very wrong and I have
dealt with that 4ever especially when I was
with Rod

I have had that issue for a very long time. I always thought that

people didn't like me, so people didn't like me. I used to say that I

would ignore it, but there is a cause and effect in every issue and situation in life. My perception of myself was everybody's reality. I was very sensitive and too trusting. I believed people would treat me how I treated them. Sometimes I did the wrong things and I got what was coming to me. But I know I tried to do right by people in any situation. If I did offend people, it was never intentional.

Privil, Koilya
```
I guess that's y my views on females are
the way they are
That's just like my crazy ass cousin
```

Liegel, Karla
```
I can understand that
Lol ☺
```

My cousin moved to Atlanta and was wild as Paris Hilton, Lindsey Lohan, and Brittany Spears all mixed into one. So imagine that. She lived with me for a while but we couldn't get along because she went out every single night. And plus she needed to get gone, I didn't want another "Diamond and her cousin situation" like in Player's Club. I had a suspicion that she was stripping but I couldn't pin that on her.

Privil, Koilya
```
My cousin wasn't like Queen but in her own
way she is
I Can't deal with the BS
That's me
```

Liegel, Karla

That's y I say that the way we act is a learned behavior, u r defensive (sometimes) because u have had to defend the way u r your whole life

Privil, Koilya

Don't get me wrong, I always had friends, but I always had a lot of haters
And Karla I believe u r Right
I want to change that defensive thing though
That's not cool

Liegel, Karla

Queen is depressed all the time because of the way she has been treated all of her life
Everyone can't be as strong as us
We are ARIES, u know

Privil, Koilya

Depression is an evil spirit
Yeah we are that….Aries…built Ford tough

Liegel, Karla

An evil spirit that can't be driven away on its own
That's where support comes into play

Privil, Koilya

Right

Liegel, Karla

That's y I take up for her
Valid actions
Not that other stuff u were talking about because I can't vouch for nonsense

Privil, Koilya
But it's emotionally draining when you have done everything you can 4 some1 or tried to help

Liegel, Karla
That's true

Privil, Koilya
And the person refuses to change because they are more comfortable being miserable

Liegel, Karla
Trust me I have been there

Privil, Koilya
Right
But Karla, my whole thing is, how could u WANT to be miserable?

Liegel, Karla
That's y I learned to tune some of it out.
I still listen, sort of, but if it affects my home life I tune it out
She has grown comfortable and accustomed to it

Privil, Koilya
Right
Because when she used to tell me about her husband, girl I found myself doing things like checking behind Vegas and all kinds of stuff
I remember telling Kali about that…

Liegel, Karla
I hate to sound like some type of psychologist but I believe that she has never really learned how to be happy and

truthfully happy. Her whole family is fake
So the feeling she knows how to feel is
depression
And I think the whole thing about being the
darkest in her family did the destruction
to her appearance issues
And I feel u on that checking Vegas thing
But I have always been a snoop
So that really didn't change anything about
me
But I did catch myself doing some things

Privil, Koilya
Exactly
U might be right about one thing
Go head young ass Dr. Karla...lol ☺

Alexander, Kali
Hey ya'll
You both are right
But I don't know who liked me or dis-liked
me
I don't care
Didn't care
And won't care

Liegel, Karla
Well I didn't get a C in psychology for
nothing
Lol ☺

Alexander, Kali
Not a C

Liegel, Karla
C+

Alexander, Kali
Oh watch out now…
But yeah…I could not entertain the bullshit
I used to ignore her
Because she would put me in a bad mood
I'll be a friend when you need one
But pity parties
I don't throw those

Privil, Koilya
Exactly Kali
That negative energy is contagious
And I don't care if someone does not like
me…because this Investment Firm and their
clients pay my bills and I have always been
that chic who will curse a chic out…don't
try me…I have calmed down a whole lot. So
Queen better be lucky!
In 15 minutes…I am out!

Alexander, Kali
Right
Mama

Privil, Koilya
Lol ☺

Alexander, Kali
I'm off
I am so lame
Sitting here talking to ya'll

Privil, Koilya
U R being Nosey

Alexander, Kali
Call me later ladies!!!

Privil, Koilya
Aight

Alexander, Kali
I will talk to ya'll later

Alexander, Kali has left the instant message conversation.

Privil, Koilya
Karla I am about to be out too
I think we should print these IM's and keep
them...we are always discussing some real
issues and good gossip...
What do u think?

Liegel, Karla
Yep
Turn it into a book
Lol ☺
Bye girl

Four of the ten commandments, deal with our relationship to God while the other six deal with our relationships with people. But all ten are about relationships. How you treat other people, not your wealth or accomplishments, is the most enduring impact you can leave on earth. –**Rick Warren**

All I know is Drama

The only thing I know is pain.
I can never determine if someone is actually being nice to me or trying to "dog" me out.
I try and I try to be the person that I know how to be, but no matter what, nothing ever works out.
Life is full of heartache.
Why do we have to endure all of this pain?
I just want to know the one person who is happy without any problems.
Maybe I could do whatever he/she is doing.
Is it me?
Is it society?
Do I set myself up for failure?
It's not even about a man anymore...
I study, but I fail the test.
I pray, but it seems as if they're never answered.
Yeah that's what it is...
And as for a man, out of all of the relationships that I have been with the only man that has showed me love is my father.
And I truly love him back.
Without a man I am lonely, with a man I am sometimes happy, sometimes miserable.
It never equals out
I have learned to live without one, but this whole life thing is unbalanced.
Maybe I need to love me more.
But as for now, all I can say is that Love and Life for most is nothing but DRAMA.

TNG

Everyone and everything around you is your teacher.
~Ken Keyers, Jr.

Chapter 3:
Disappointments

Life isn't always going to bring you spring days and summer weather.

-Tawana Necole

Have you not heard about that thing us white guys do?
-Matt Lesson

Karla may have been on to something when she said to turn our conversations into a book, but Karla and Kali weren't saving the conversations. So I took it upon myself to start saving them. Anyone I spoke with through the PC or IM was going to be a character in this bright idea of a book. They just didn't know it. And to think my minor in Journalism would go to waste! So I started with Matt Lesson. Matt was the recruiter that helped us land the job with the Investment Firm. He was always pleasant with me. I always knew he liked me but I never entertained the idea because he was married to a blonde Exec making a whole lot of dough! Nevertheless, she ended up leaving him. He called me and talked to me all about it one day. He was heart broken because she called it off and she told him it wasn't another guy, but he knew better. He just didn't want to admit it.

Matt and I were really good friends and he even invited me out to Rays on the River (a popular seafood restaurant in Atlanta) once. We had a great time. I played naïve about him having a crush on me but that night was wonderful. There was a jazz singer and she was great. Matt kept ordering me all of this wine trying to get me twisted but it didn't work. I knew Matt's situation and I didn't want to be caught in a situation with Matt and his wife. I didn't want to entertain the thought of him having to kill me to get rid of me so he could be with his true love. So I always knew to keep it professional with Matt. He could only respect me for that.

Vegas sort of had an idea that Matt liked me. Especially when he found out that we went to dinner. I tried to play it off like he was giving me some recruiting tips but he didn't fall all the way for it. Vegas was smart and too busy doing things he had no business doing to worry about what I was doing or what was going on in my life. Nothing changed about Vegas after we started living together with the baby. The same things he was doing in Savannah, he was doing in Atlanta. He wasn't gone as much during the week, but he was ghost on the weekends. And yes Austin Ronald Goodyear, Jr. was our baby's name.

April 17, 2005

Lesson, Matt
I bet you thought I fell off the face of the earth.

Privil, Koilya
Actually I knew you left the company
I didn't want to call you because I didn't want to seem like I was prying...
I know all is well with u though.

Lesson, Matt
It was a very sudden thing
I had an offer that I could not turn down
I start the new job in a week
In the meantime, I have been working on a contract recruiting job for a friend here in Atlanta

In my 18 months with the Investment Firm,
I've had 5 managers
My new job will have me back on the road so
that will be fun
I will miss the special people that I met
at the Firm...
That means you

Privil, Koilya
Ahh...We will stay in touch. I may be leaving
in a couple months as well.

Lesson, Matt
Your Boyfriend or the Investment firm?
Ahahahahaha

Privil, Koilya
BOTH! I am so sick and tired of that man!

Lesson, Matt
Sorry he is not treating you right.

Privil, Koilya
He's stupid, lame, dump and thinks I won't
leave or cheat on him!

Lesson, Matt
Dump?

Privil, Koilya
U know what I mean, Dumb!!!

Lesson, Matt
You wouldn't want to leave my house...

Privil, Koilya
I bet I wouldn't

Lesson, Matt
You would be too spoiled in no time

Privil, Koilya
I knew you had a thing for me...

Lesson, Matt
Always

Privil, Koilya
Matt...that's all I can say

Lesson, Matt
Keep my number in your file for a BC.
404-999-4349

Privil, Koilya
Ok

Lesson, Matt
You have no idea what I am talking about do you?

Privil, Koilya
No, I just agreed

I knew exactly what he was talking about, but I was not about to take it there with him on the work computer! Seriously, Matt, a Booty Call? With you? NO!

Lesson, Matt
You should never do that with me...hahahahaha
You may end up in my hot tub at the crib

Privil, Koilya
I am a big girl 25 in a couple days
I can definitely handle you
I have been this long

Lesson, Matt
You are all grown up that is for sure ☺

Privil, Koilya
Yeah with so many responsibilities
I wish I was a kid again...

Lesson, Matt
Come up one night and I will cook you
dinner.

Privil, Koilya
What happened to your girlfriend?

Now Matt was getting BOLD! What the hell??? He was coming on super strong and I had to calm his ass down before it got too far. I didn't want to hurt his feelings but he was trying to get the booty and I saw right through it all.

Lesson, Matt
I just date
I am not looking to get married again
anytime soon

Privil, Koilya
I know
Have you ever dated an African American
woman?

Lesson, Matt
Once

Privil, Koilya
How was it?

Matt knew he never dated a black woman and he was trying to be cool about it. But I knew better from his answer and also because I never got a response that day.

****

April 18, 2005

Lesson, Matt
```
I should ask you if you have ever been to
the "light side"
```

Privil, Koilya
```
Yes
But he never wanted to commit
```

Look at how he tried to switch it around on me. Matt was so sweet and down to earth, but I could never see him being my "down-low" friend or man for that matter. I will never forget Rod and all he taught me. Dating him was an extraordinary experience. But we are still really good friends. After we found out that Vegas fathered AJ, Rod vowed to me that we would remain friends and once every couple months, we would hang out with each other to catch up.

Lesson, Matt
```
Girl, you would be putty in my
hands...hahahahahahahahahahahahahahaha
Have you not heard about that thing us
white guys do?
Ha ha ha ha
```

Privil, Koilya
Matt, u r a mess!

Lesson, Matt
I would have to agree with you Koilya
I can't wait to get back out on the road
I'm going to Sacramento on the 29th for a
week
How's John?

Privil, Koilya
Who is John? My baby's name is AJ

Lesson, Matt
Typo my bad...

Privil, Koilya
Not a typo...he is going to be 1 next month
Can you believe we have known each other
that long?

Lesson, Matt
Yeah that is a long time
Just wait until he gets into his terrible
two's

Privil, Koilya
That means I will be 26...
I would like to be accomplished by then
with my goals and aspirations...
I feel like I am getting so OLD
And nothing I really want to do is being
done!

Lesson, Matt
Most likely I will be on the road
We'll see
Hopefully in San Diego

Privil, Koilya
```
So your new job has you traveling all over
I am so jealous
```

Lesson, Matt
```
I will be racking up the miles.
Most of it will be West Coast and Southwest
Right now I am working a contract
recruiting job for a friend over off of S
Atlanta Road.
```

After Matt saw that trying to hit on me was getting him nowhere, that was the end of him pursuing me. He didn't even remember my baby's name! So why would I date someone like that. I haven't talked to old Matt since that day.

Now Greg was one of the cutest and sexiest thangs that walked the floors of the Investment Firm. He was light brown with jet black hair. The fact that he was so laid back and cool didn't add to me sometimes lusting after him. You felt a cool breeze when he walked by. He tried to date Kali but it didn't work out. Kali thought he was lame and she always said that he was not her type. She claims that he tried to get the "goods" when he came over after work one night. He bought her a bottle of champagne to celebrate her birthday and after watching a movie or two and drinking almost the whole bottle, he went in for the bait. Kali said that's what turned her off. So their relationship (on that level) ended for the most part. *So she says...*

I started to become Greg's work crush after I returned from maternity leave. I guess he really couldn't see what I was working with being all fat and pregnant. The brotha laid low, observed my style, and then finally stepped to me. Because I was a loyal friend, I told Kali that Greg tried to take me out. Of course she said to me what every female says knowing they don't mean it, "Girl it's all good, we didn't hit it off. It's cool with me." But because I am a very selfish woman, I could never talk to Greg or go out with him for that matter. I was second to Kali. From learned mistakes in the past, I vowed to myself that I would always be number one when it came to men in my life. I just flirted with him at work but knew deep down it could and would never be anything.

****

April 19, 2005

Privil, Koilya
I need help please
Hello manager on duty

Reid, Greg
22nd floor only...Lol ☺

Privil, Koilya
Lol ☺ I used to sit right by you!
So u wouldn't come down here to help me?

Reid, Greg
Of course
Anytime

Privil, Koilya
You don't even holla at your work crush anymore...
U know Kali is coming back?

Reid, Greg
I tried to get with u but u never hollered
back…

Privil, Koilya
Yes I did!

Reid, Greg
I know u were busy with your spoken
word/poetry and writing

Privil, Koilya
Whatever
How r u going to adapt when Kali comes
back?
That's the million dollar question!

Reid, Greg
The same
I haven't spoke to Kali in a minute
We are cool but that's it
I was never Kali's type

Privil, Koilya
Kali is picky about EVERYTHING
So I totally understand
When are we going 4 drinks?
This weekend would be perfect
My baby is leaving today

Reid, Greg
U TELL ME
U have been ducking me like the flu

Privil, Koilya
Lol ☺

Reid, Greg
This weekend is cool

Privil, Koilya
Is your number still the same?

Reid, Greg
Yep

Privil, Koilya
R U working tomorrow?

Reid, Greg
Naw

Privil, Koilya
Do u want to go tomorrow after I get my
hair done
I have a 6:30 appt…
So I am going to be extra fly

Reid, Greg
That's cool
Intermezzos?

Privil, Koilya
So I'll call u
My number is still the same
The Intermezzos downtown would be perfect

Reid, Greg
That's what's up

Privil, Koilya
Don't stand me up!

Reid, Greg
I should be telling u that

Privil, Koilya
I would NEVER!
Lol ☺

Reid, Greg
Uh huh...

Privil, Koilya
Talk to u then handsome...
u need to tell me what's up with your
business

Reid, Greg
Of course...I still want to hear your
writing...
I want some copies of your pics too...
U was looking oh so good

Privil, Koilya
Whatever
I haven't talked to u since u saw them pics
I lost some of my work
Can u believe that?
I cant...
Too blowed
But I will make sure u hear some of my
material
I'll c what I can do about the copies

Reid, Greg
Wow...Somebody stole your material...
Who r u talking about for publication???
I know some cats
I'll see if I can a get some contact info
by tomorrow to give u...

Privil, Koilya
Thank u
I need to holla at you about the whole
situation n-e way
But we'll talk tomorrow
I am out!

Greg and I ended up not going out because Sabrina took too long to style my hair. So if I went out with him, it would have been suspicious. I was slick and was not about to get caught with a dude that was trying to holla at all the chic's in the office. Through office gossip, I heard he tried to take all of the cute girls out for drinks. Guys don't like an around the way girl and I don't like a guy who tries to date everybody! I like the guys I date to be selective. One thing Vegas was NOT going to do, was catch me cheating. I was on the verge of falling into another man's arm, but I still didn't want it to be Greg's. He was a play boy and a bachelor who played the game. When Sharlene told me that she actually went out with him, I was completely turned off.

Sharlene was my co-worker turned friend from up north. Over time, we grew close. She was an Assistant VP to the Client Managers. She was the person that booked all of the appointments for the Managers and if the clients had a fraudulent issue, she assigned those cases as well. She recently was promoted to handle the work load of the department.

****

April 20, 2005

Privil, Koilya
Did u find someone to go to Miami with u?

Liegel, Karla
No

Privil, Koilya
So when r u leaving?
Did u get the funds?

Leigel, Karla
They are pending...Lol ☺

Privil, Koilya
Lol ☺ Pending
U R so crazy!!!

Liegel, Karla
Lol ☺
Granddaddy authorized $350
And the other sponsor authorized $150

Now Karla was all about getting her bills and extra-curricular paid by men. She always had a new hustle or man to take care of her bills, but she wasn't going about it the right way. She was messing with some *old* Jamaican man that had a lot of money. He was separated from his wife and would pick up the young chics that hung out at Scores by "caking" them for about a month or two. I told Karla not to mess with that old-rusty Jamaican because he may have been a lose canon. But Karla wasn't afraid to ask. I couldn't ask a man for money! That was just off limits. It's a BIG difference if they offer it or if they are generous. But asking is so not classy to me.

Alexander, Kali is starting this conversation with the message:
I have a sick child to deal with and it is not fun!
But I did get my hair done yesterday
I was in and out in one hour

Karla was talking to Kali about being tardy to work and she used her child every chance she could to get out of coming to work or being there on time. I was mute because I didn't want to hear the excuses.

Liegel, Karla
Lol ☺
U R A mess
I need to get the $ by Sunday so I can know
for sure that I am going
I don't need anybody setting me up

Alexander, Kali
Right.
You better cook for that man!
Tuna melt!

Liegel, Karla
Lol ☺
The only thing he wants is a hug
So he says...
I can do that all day

Alexander, Kali
Just a hug?

Liegel, Karla
YEA
SO HE SAYS...

Privil, Koilya
I had to catch up
That man might put roots on u Karla
No hugs

Alexander, Kali
What are roots?

Privil, Koilya
Girl u never heard of roots?

Alexander, Kali
No I don't think so

Privil, Koilya
Girl Jamaicans and Carolina/Indians
Practice witch craft

Liegel, Karla
Koilya u would know
Lol ☺

Privil, Koilya
Lol ☺
Girl

Liegel, Karla
ROOTS?
WTH?

Privil, Koilya
I could never sleep out because my father
said that people would do that crazy stuff
Roots…
Jamaicans do it too

Alexander, Kali
Quit being scary Koilya!

Privil, Koilya
Lol ☺
The good girl always comes out
U R crazy Kali
Talking about I am scary

Liegel, Karla
Lol ☺

Privil, Koilya
Ya'll our book is going to be off the chain

Liegel, Karla
Lol ☺ Yep

Privil, Koilya
Even convos that you all have with guys
Save them
Or print them
Each day we need to designate somebody

Alexander, Kali
Koilya can't drink at Frequency
I'm over here jamming
UGK, Jeezy, Crime Mob
WHAT!

Liegel, Karla
So

Alexander, Kali
Jealous
You should have a pre-drinking gathering
before you go out
And have everyone should bring a bottle

Liegel, Karla
We are
U are so late

Karla always threw parties, cookouts, events, or anything that involved people coming over, eating, dancing, playing cards, or just having a good old fashioned time.

Liegel, Karla
Everyone is meeting at my house

Alexander, Kali
Oh...send out the invite
Today is Friday

Liegel, Karla
I am not inviting that many people

Alexander, Kali
Well you did not invite me

Liegel, Karla
Yes I did
U were the one talking about your funds
Remember

Alexander, Kali
I know...I can't forget that

Kali was full of it. She never went out with us. We never understood if it was because she wanted *all* the attention to herself or what. She was selfish. I do know that for sure. She wanted her name to be somewhere all up in the mix of things. I remember we all planned to go out. Karla and I had to wait on Kali to find a babysitter. Well, the babysitter came and she called the both of us and told us she was on the way. This was about 9:30 PM. We waited so long, we both fell asleep. It was about 12:30 AM when Karla called me and asked if I spoke to Kali. We didn't hear from Kali that night. The next day she claims she got lost, but Karla and I both knew that was a lie. She wanted to trick off with one of her guy friends and that was cool, but why stand us up? All she had to do was say that. So we stopped inviting her to things. If she didn't make excuses why she couldn't come to an event, she said she would come, and would never show up. Kali could be really shady at times but then super cool. I don't know what her problem was, but I started to dislike some of the things she would do. I have always been vocal and honest, but Kali had insecurity issues about herself. It seemed like some of the characteristics that she lacked; she envied in others but tried to keep those people close to her.

Alexander, Kali
Ya'll I'm in love

Liegel, Karla
Whatever
With who
NOW...LOL ☺

Alexander, Kali
I am...Tony

Liegel, Karla
?

Alexander, Kali
Grand Hustle

Liegel, Karla
Step away
Lol ☺

"Grand Hustle" was the nick name of this guy that Kali was falling head over heels in love with. We called him "Grand Hustle" because when Kali first met him he told her that he worked at T.I's studio. Now we don't know how true that was, because he stayed locked up more than a little. But that's how he got the nickname.

Liegel, Karla
Y now
What did he do?

Alexander, Kali
He fixed my brakes

Liegel, Karla
I thought so
Lol ☺
That would have done it for me too

Alexander, Kali
But this truck he was in yesterday...would have done it too

Liegel, Karla
Lol ☺
Alright groupie

Alexander, Kali
No...no...no...I can't help it he has nice cars...
But it is an added benefit
The rims were so beautiful...26's

Kali and Karla were shallow when it came to certain things. If a guy fixed my brakes, yes that would have definitely been an added benefit but that would not make me "fall in love." I realize that some people don't mature because they lack experience. I went to college and Kali and Karla didn't. So sometimes our views were different. I never held that against them and I respect them as mothers, but sometimes it was like talking to a brick wall.

Privil, Koilya
```
I knew Grand Hustle was the one 4 u
U the scary one
U got him right where u want him...
He likes u...
I told u that b4
And you better come to Karla's tomorrow
And I WILL have a glass of wine at
Frequency
Momma
```

Alexander, Kali
```
I have to check the funds...
I really want to come
Grand hustle isn't feeling me like that...
what he does for me is chomp change
I think he might like me a little though
```

Privil, Koilya
```
He still looked out 4 u
He makes sure u get 2 work
```

Alexander, Kali
```
Right
But he told me...he will NOT pay my rent
But he can help on the bills
```

Liegel, Karla
Well money is money. Rent or bills
Every lil' bit helps
U need to see what he is feeling
But don't scare him though
U know he's a thug

Privil, Koilya
She's afraid to open up

Liegel, Karla
Yea

Privil, Koilya
Scared to be affectionate

Liegel, Karla
Yep

Alexander, Kali
But that is why I like him...he is the one
that bought that to light about me (not
opening up and being affectionate)
Is your best friend sister going out Karla?
I like her...she seems fun...

Liegel, Karla
She is crazy
Lol ☺
She may
She normally does
But I don't know

Alexander, Kali
What would I wear?
Do ya'll watch Charm School?
I like that show...
Hello?
Ya'll are boring

We were working. We couldn't sit around, listen to music, and talk all day like Kali. All she was doing was working with the interns.

Liegel, Karla
```
I texted my best friend about what u said
and she was like her sister said the same
thing
She said ya'll are Lesbos
Lol ☺
```

Alexander, Kali
```
Hey I know cool people when I see them
```

Liegel, Karla
```
Lol ☺
Yea u know me
```

Privil, Koilya
```
I like Charm School
But did u notice most of the girls got
implants
After Flavor of Love
```

That was just not cool to me. The whole dating reality TV show was entertaining, but the integrity of the women on the show were compromised and conformed to "Sex Sells." And that is what has so many young females thinking it is ok to swing on a pole or casually have sex. I am not knocking anyone's hustle or how they make their money, but people need to start to think about their role on earth. Ultimately, our character/soul will outlive everything. Through my actions and now that I know better, I want to always be a positive role model. I would never want to be responsible for helping a young female make a decision on being a stripper. I don't knock the hustle, I just wouldn't want someone to make that decision based off of my actions. There are so many ways to hustle and I want to provide that option to females. I wouldn't want to be the cause of young girls contracting HIV because they see me on TV engaging in casual sex and think that it's ok. I wouldn't want them feeling insecure about their body because I was insecure about mine. That's the point I am trying to make. Yes, reality TV is very entertaining, but so misleading. The females that are chosen for the shows portray African American Women in a very negative light. I hope that this book I am writing is going to change that one chic at a time.

Privil, Koilya
Karla tell your best friend not to bring
her sisters' boyfriend!!!
Herpes mouth!

Liegel, Karla
Lol ☺

Alexander, Kali
Stop Koilya

Karla's best friend sister, Michelle, was a real sista. She was fun and older than all of us, and she knew how to have a good time. But that "boo" of hers just could never control himself. While playing cards one night, at one of Karla's cookouts, he thumped me on my butt and thought the shit was cool. So ever since then I had a very bad taste in my mouth about him.

Alexander, Kali
```
It is a free country
He wouldn't be the only person in there
with it
I'm sure
Be nice
```

Liegel, Karla
```
Lol ☺
True
But he is a DAWG
```

Privil, Koilya
```
I was wrong
I can admit
```

Liegel, Karla
```
Lol ☺
```

Privil, Koilya
```
She can bring him...
Lol ☺
She better bring a leash though
Or they will be fighting in Frequency
And Then What
```

Liegel, Karla
```
Michelle said she doesn't have any funds
Just like her twin Kali
```

Alexander, Kali
So what
Times are hard

Liegel, Karla
I'm ready to go
Like
ASAP

Alexander, Kali
What time do you get off today?

Liegel, Karla
7pm
I'm so ready to go I can cry

Privil, Koilya
Don't u know I was with a client for a 1
hour and 30 minutes/these clients make me
sick…so demanding!
I missed lunch and everything!
I am blowed and hungry

Liegel, Karla
Lol ☺ What man?

Privil, Koilya
Older guy from NJ
He talked my head off!

Liegel, Karla
Lol ☺

Privil, Koilya
I am so ready for tomorrow
I invited my crush
I hope he has some cute friends
Cause he is too cute!
Goodness

Don't know what I got myself into talking
to a hood dude from Atlanta

I was searching for love in all the wrong places just like Karla.
After AJ was born, Vegas moved to Atlanta and was doing his
own thang. He didn't work because he felt like he was above that.
He was still living that "perception" type lifestyle but blowing his
money on B.S. I loved being a working mom. I couldn't sit
around, shop, or attend Country Club meetings with snobbish
women that didn't know anything about life and the importance
of living it to the fullest. I always knew my life had a purpose, so
I didn't mind working. I didn't go to college just because and I
continued my education.

Because we had been away from one another while Vegas lived
in Savannah, we grew apart but still tried to make our
relationship work. AJ was the link to our destiny together. We
held on to empty hope for so long. All of the things that Vegas
did to get me, stopped all together. He was away from home
constantly. He claims he was taking care of business. I was so
hurt because of the way I was being treated. Since he refused to
leave, even after the arguments and fights, I was going to take it
upon myself to force him to leave. Some of the rumors that were
being said about him robbing folks, was starting to look true. I
found things in the house that only people who lived that type of
lifestyle would use. When I would ask him about it, he would

always deny any involvement. I always reminded him we were too blessed to be ignorant.

Shit hit the fan when his two friends were murdered and he was the only witness to what actually happened. My college sweetheart was into selling drugs and robbing folks. It was true and I didn't want to believe it. I ignored all the signs and I constantly looked at the potential guy Vegas was or could be. I still to this day cannot understand why he engaged in that lifestyle! The detective that knocked on my door explained to me that the Feds were watching him and his friends for two years. The phones were tapped and even though they used "codes & "slang" the detectives used a snitch to decode everything. The last incident involved a fifty pound drug deal with some guys from Detroit. Vegas and his crew heard that the guys from Detroit were going to rob them. So Vegas and his homeboys came up with this plan to meet the Detroit crew a day later with the work/drugs. Vegas thought that they would get away like a fat rat by keeping the drugs and stealing the money for the drugs from the guys from Detroit. Well, the guys that Vegas and his friends were selling to or were going to rob were a day ahead of them. I say they met their match. These guys apparently were in the same type of business Vegas and his crew were into but had a better plan strategically. I personally think that the snitch that the detectives were using caused this horrific crime and he may have been apart of Vegas' crew. The guys didn't strike until Vegas and his friends had the drugs. While stopped at a red light on the way back to Atlanta, the dudes opened fire with 8k's and killed his two friends on the spot. Vegas was in the back seat and managed not to get shot but had some minor bruises and cuts because the car ran head on to another car after the driver was murdered. After that incident, Vegas was not the same.

All of our assets were seized and a lien was placed on all of our money. I should have NEVER opened an account with a guy that I was *shacking* with! All of the money that I was supposed to get for my 25th birthday was placed on hold and there was nothing I could do about it. I didn't tell Ann about this situation, because again, she had endured so much with my brother and father. I knew eventually I would be able to get the funds that were rightfully mine, but the DA had to determine what was legit on Vegas' accounts and my accounts. Back pay was going to be lovely when it was finally released to us and I was definitely going to get a lawyer to sue them for holding me up; forcing me into almost poverty, but that was all going to take a while. I was living off of my paychecks and that was no fun. I always had a jacked up mentality about money and not having any; my worse fear came knocking on my door when this situation occurred. The key to getting through a crisis with your mate will be determined on how you view any situation. Who you are defines everything around you and what you are about. I was in a relationship with a man that did not have good morals. He was a thief. Ann always told me when you steal; you lie. I started to think that maybe the money that was in his account was all a front because his grandfather was into the gangsta type lifestyle. I had to do some investigating at work without losing my job. Vegas had to be the front man for these actions. His friends didn't have any money but he was guaranteed to beat the case because no one could testify against him…unless somebody could rise from being dead.

I had to understand that when you are in a relationship, it's a compromise; give and take. If you aren't willing to do that for your spouse, then you will have serious problems. Your character is always up against your reputation. A person's character should represent integrity. Do what's right in any situation in your life and the outcome will be positive. Vegas had to relearn all of these important concepts and I had to help teach him that lesson. He was forced to get a job while this whole situation worked itself out and I was on the search for love.

Liegel, Karla
Koilya u a mess
Lol ☺
Did he say he was going to come?

Privil, Koilya
No
We'll see

Liegel, Karla
O ok

Alexander, Kali
Who is this crush?
I thought you were married?

Privil, Koilya
Jose
Josephina in my phone
If I was married, I wouldn't be talking to
buddy or trying to talk to him
Vegas needs to step it up
I am tired of playing house

Liegel, Karla
Lol ☺
I feel u

Privil, Koilya
Make it official or don't expect me to be
totally committed

Liegel, Karla
Marry Me!
Lol ☺

Privil, Koilya
Lol ☺

Liegel, Karla
AMEN

Privil, Koilya
U crazy

Liegel, Karla
PREACH!

Privil, Koilya
And then we have little AJ
And I just went through all of that drama!

Liegel, Karla
LOL ☺
CHURCH
LOL ☺

Privil, Koilya
Come on now
U know if u want to be with me or not

Liegel, Karla
RIGHT
Rather its today or tomorrow he knows

Alexander, Kali
Right

Liegel, Karla
He is just procrastinating

Alexander, Kali
I need a ring

Liegel, Karla
She has one

Alexander, Kali
Engagement?

Liegel, Karla
I thought so
KOILYA?

Alexander, Kali
?

Liegel, Karla
```
??????????????????
Lol ☺
```

Alexander, Kali
```
Lol ☺
Jon wants to join our conversation
```

Jon was this intern that Kali worked with. Karla knew him from school and I guess he was really curious about what we were talking about since Kali was running her mouth and telling my business to him.

Alexander, Kali
```
He wants to meddle
Oh and he claims he is going to Frequency
on Saturday
He also claims his cousin has a pad in
Buckhead
```

Privil, Koilya
```
What does he have to say?
Trying to be in our book!
```

Alexander, Kali
```
Right
```

Liegel, Karla
```
He ain't getting no $
Lol ☺
```

Privil, Koilya
```
Lol ☺
None
```

Liegel, Karla
But he can join the conversation

Privil, Koilya
No proceeds

Liegel, Karla
Lol ☺

Alexander, Kali
Ya'll silly ☺

Jon Hooder has been added to the instant message conversation.

Alexander, Kali
Who invited him?

Jon Hooder has left the instant message conversation.

Privil, Koilya
U did

Liegel, Karla
Lol ☺
He's gone

Alexander, Kali
No I did not!

Liegel, Karla
I did
Lol ☺

Privil, Koilya
KARLA!
Lol ☺
And then u r trying to be all slick

Hooder, Jon has been added to the instant message conversation.

Liegel, Karla
Kali did this time

Liegel, Karla
Lol ☺

Liegel, Karla
Hey Jon

Alexander, Kali
Yeah

Liegel, Karla
Just trying to be nosey

Privil, Koilya
He doesn't want to be in a convo with all
these women

Liegel, Karla
Lol ☺

Alexander, Kali
Yeah he does

Liegel, Karla
Yes he does
He's a PLAYA
LOL ☺

Alexander, Kali
He thinks he is a pimp

Liegel, Karla
NOT!
LOL ☺

Privil, Koilya
```
Lol ☺
Lol ☺
```

Alexander, Kali
```
He's training & can't type right now
```

Liegel, Karla
```
He isn't saying anything
LAME
```

Alexander, Kali
```
You know "the eyes" are always watching
```

Kali's boss was "the eyes." She was so intimidated by Kali. She did everything in her power to make Kali miserable. But Kali, stuck it out. I think that is why she so desperately wanted to come back to the department we all started together.

Privil, Koilya
```
Kali
I had a ring but I lost it
Remember the ring
I was showing in the beauty shop?
```

Liegel, Karla
```
O my
```

Privil, Koilya
```
I lost it
```

Liegel, Karla
```
Ooooooooooooooooooo
```

Alexander, Kali
I've been sitting over here chilling

Liegel, Karla
Lol ☺

Alexander, Kali
Interns needing my help and everything

Liegel, Karla
Ooooo

Privil, Koilya
U definitely gonna get in trouble from that witch

Liegel, Karla
Oops

Privil, Koilya
Her BA

We couldn't say what we wanted but B.A. = Bitch Ass

Liegel, Karla
Lol ☺
I got that
Lol ☺

Privil, Koilya
Lol ☺
I can't say it all the way

Liegel, Karla
I know what u mean

Hooder, Jon
Karla what's up buddy?

Alexander, Kali
Girl that crazy boy that I went out with
the other night gave me your ring. ☺

Privil, Koilya
Do u remember that ring though?

Alexander, Kali
Yeah

Privil, Koilya
Girl I can NOT find it anywhere!
So maybe we are supposed to wait
Or not be together...1 of the 2

Liegel, Karla
Hey Jon
How have u been?

Hooder, Jon
I have been good

Liegel, Karla
And Koilya does he know that u lost the
ring?
U better not stand us up on Saturday Jon
U know how u do
And tell lemon head to call me

Alexander, Kali
RIGHT!

Privil, Koilya
Vegas thinks I pawned it
But I told him it was lost

Liegel, Karla
Well he just needs to buy you another
one...so was it an engagement ring or
not...inquiring minds want to know

Privil, Koilya
It was NOT an engagement ring
I got it for my 24th b-day
He has me another one
I can go to Helzberg and pick out which
ever ring I want
He claims that he has been paying on a ring
since Feb
But I haven't done that....and I don't know
if I want to
He needs to get his self together

Alexander, Kali
SN: Why does Maurice keep trying to get me
to come over his house?

Maurice was one of Kali's old friends who worked at the Firm
with us. Maurice was feeling Kali, but again it wasn't reciprocal.
Maurice thought he was so slick, but I knew he was trying to be a
little player on the low. The sad part about it was that he was
really a *great* guy. His mother raised him respectful. He had
manners and I never saw him act outside of his character, but for
some reason he carried a loaded glock. That gun went
everywhere with him. Kali said she didn't know why he carried it
because he was just a regular old cat, but I knew better. Maurice
fell hard for Kali and if just being her friend was all she wanted,
he respected that. But when I think about it Maurice always

wanted chics that he could not have or who were already taken. I knew that he was trying to hook up with Sharlene but due to a conflict of interests concerning friends, I kept my mouth shut. Besides the two of them weren't friends. I guess some guys just like to deal with women who they don't have to fully commit too. But then again Kali wasn't taken. So I don't know what his MO was.

Liegel, Karla
Lol ☺
He is a mess
I told him about the club

Privil, Koilya
And Kali u r right he is lame

Liegel, Karla
Lol ☺

Hooder, Jon
Karla I would never do that to u

Privil, Koilya
With that banana game he was trying to get us to play at your house the other night Karla

Liegel, Karla
Lol ☺

Privil, Koilya
He is lame
Lol ☺

Liegel, Karla
And yes u would Jon

Privil, Koilya
He likes u Kali
He was all in your face the entire night

Liegel, Karla
Jon U know u are always reneging

Privil, Koilya
I kept asking myself y does Kali say that
Maurice is lame?

Alexander, Kali
He Keeps sending me IM's talking about I
thought you was going out with me this
weekend

Privil, Koilya
No...
Beat It Maurice!

Liegel, Karla
I don't know why he kept talking about he's
gonna get us loose...

Maurice and his friends came over to Karla's get together and we were all having a good time. But they were trying to take some chics home with them. They didn't know we were not new to the game. I know I wasn't some little dumb chic that would let it all hang out with guys that I wasn't interested in. Maurice tried to get us to play some stupid drinking game and that is not cool in my book. I am grown with a child. When a woman meets a guy, she knows if she is going to let him get some or not. I'd rather a guy just be honest and say what he wants and then allow me to make my own decision if I want to have sex or mess around with him like that. I hate when guys try to make the decision for me and that was super lame in our book!

Alexander, Kali
Right...go home...Maurice with yo lame @ss

Privil, Koilya
Sipping on the Grey Goose all night

Liegel, Karla
Lol ☺

Alexander, Kali
My Grey Goose

Privil, Koilya
Lol ☺
A cup full

Liegel, Karla
And we were taking shots like the big dogs

Privil, Koilya
His cup was still filled when they left

Liegel, Karla
Man up Maurice
Lol ☺

Privil, Koilya
Lol ☺

Alexander, Kali
He bought that cheap stuff

Liegel, Karla
What did he bring?
Other than his homeboys

Hooder, Jon
Ya'll be easy ladies I am out

Hooder, Jon has left the instant message conversation.

Alexander, Kali
That frosted Brandy...Christian Brothers

Privil, Koilya
Lol ☺
Christian bro is straight
But not no old man Brandy
Or is that the same

Alexander, Kali
It's the same Koilya

Privil, Koilya
Lol ☺
Well he can slide because of the name

I didn't know anything about alcohol. I was a weed smoker and
wine drinker, not alcoholic or pill popper.

Liegel, Karla
Lol ☺
Jon left
Convo to intense or because we were making
jokes out of Maurice?

We should invite more men to the
conversations

Privil, Koilya
To get there input

Liegel, Karla
Yea
Somebody that's not scary

Privil, Koilya
Jon was scary

Liegel, Karla
He had NO COMMENT

Privil, Koilya
He was reading and laughing

Liegel, Karla
Right

Privil, Koilya
He'll probably say something to his home
boyz

I've learned that guys gossip *way* more than girls. Just watch

ESPN. That channel is their soap opera. The commentators will

turn the smallest little incident into something big so they can

have an opinion about it.

Liegel, Karla
Right
We need some input
Not PROOFREADERS
LOL ☺

Privil, Koilya
Especially about our situations

Liegel, Karla
RIGHT
The name of the Book should be
REAL TALK
What people really have to say about the
workplace

Privil, Koilya
No! Let's call it Corporate Chics
And Chics without the K
So it could be our own thing
We got swag, we are stylish, we are smart
and from different walks of life
Kali's Mexican and Karla you are damn near
white!
And then we can turn this book into a show!

We had Big Dreams and Ideas but really didn't know that we

could capitalize on them. I saw the vision of this book. It stuck

with me and would not go away.

Liegel, Karla
Right.
Karla I am not white….
Lol ☺
I am mixed
Thank you very much

Privil, Koilya
Ok Karla whatever you say
And while other people are working

We will be going on shows marketing the
book
And making money!!!

Liegel, Karla
$$$$$$$$$$$

**Hooder, Jon has been added to the instant message
conversation.**

Alexander, Kali
Jon said he isn't scary
And Koilya I am not Mexican!
I am Puerto Rican

Liegel, Karla
Whatever Jon
And yes get Kali get her together
With her Indian @ss
Lol ☺

Alexander, Kali
He wanted me to add him back to the chat

Liegel, Karla
Well prove yoself

Alexander, Kali
I'm about to get loose like Maurice and his
friends thought they were gonna get us to
do
LOL ☺
But in another way, I am out!

Liegel, Karla
Bye

Alexander, Kali has left the instant message conversation

Hooder, Jon
Scary who

Privil, Koilya
Lol ☺
Karla u see your boy?
And I am half Native American...FYI
I am out Karla...I'll call u
Nice to meet u Jon
****

April 24, 2005

Privil, Koilya
Karla I didn't know u worked today
All of these clients!!!
Where did they come from?

Liegel, Karla
Girl, yes I'm here...
And ready to go

Alexander, Kali
I wanted some Waffle House so bad this
morning

Liegel, Karla
We had some...And It was good

Alexander, Kali
I am about to start planning my birthday
party

Liegel, Karla
What r u thinking of doing?

Alexander, Kali
Definitely the Body Tap thing
I think that would be fun

135

Kali always had some bright idea for something. Ever since Tiny (T.I.'s wife) and Monica had a birthday party for their boyfriends at the strip club she thought this was such a good idea.

Alexander, Kali
And maybe a BBQ

Liegel, Karla
Sounds good to me

Alexander, Kali
Its going be packed on that weekend
If we go to Body Tap, I would like it to be
a large group

Liegel, Karla
Yea

Alexander, Kali
I want it to be crowded…
I'm gonna pin money on me…
so that people will add on…
I want a party Dress
Like Tocarra has on in that email I sent
you
Did you see the pictures?
Are you all still busy?

Liegel, Karla
All day we are busy
I saw the pics
That's too dressy Kali

Alexander, Kali
No…You think?

Liegel, Karla
Uh yes

Privil, Koilya
Hot mess
This dept...
Kali you may want to stay where u r

Liegel, Karla
No mam
I doubt it
The internship program may be worse than
here
Girl yo boy keep sending Instant Messages

Karla was talking about this new guy who she was possibly

interested in from the Firm. She was always interested in

somebody new!!!

Liegel, Karla
He said we should have done this earlier

Privil, Koilya
What!
He is really a good guy!
I hope "something" comes of it

Liegel, Karla
Me too
Lil Akon
Lol ☺

Privil, Koilya
Yeah the tall version
Cute too

Liegel, Karla
Tall dark and handsome…Baby!
Lol ☺

Privil, Koilya
Lol ☺
U R crazy

Alexander, Kali
Who?
I want to know!
Liegel, Karla
Carlton Bailey

Alexander, Kali
Oh…he's really nice
That's my buddy
He was in the Internship program
We went out to Dugans once in our department
He's very fun & loving
But call me later….I'm OUT!
****

April 25, 2005

Alexander, Kali
Good Morning

Privil, Koilya
Hey Miss Lady
U R late

Alexander, Kali
I work 10-2 today

Privil, Koilya
Cool
That's a really cool schedule

Alexander, Kali
Yeah...but you have to work on Saturdays to get it

Privil, Koilya
Oh
Only 4 hours?

Alexander, Kali
Yeah

Privil, Koilya
That's not bad either
Did u hear anything from our old manager, Sarah?

Alexander, Kali
No but my manager said I can't leave or apply for another job until June

Privil, Koilya
What!

Alexander, Kali
I'm going to call Sarah and see if there is anything that I can do

Privil, Koilya
No...
Your manager is Evil

Alexander, Kali
She is saying because I have a write up

Privil, Koilya
She is still Evil
Your manager can hold you back
My manager didn't do it to me
But upper management did

So certain managers are going to try and stop u from moving up or around

Alexander, Kali
Where were you going to go?
Upper management...are you talking about Sarah?

Privil, Koilya
Yes
I applied for the Senior Client Manager & Training position
And didn't get it
It's all good
No money was involved but the principle of the whole situation is crazy

Alexander, Kali
Right
Did they give you the reason for holding you back?

Privil, Koilya
My interviewing skills didn't paint the picture of a leader even though they know I have the qualities and skills
????
WTF!
???

Alexander, Kali
???

Sarah was the manager in the pilot department but recently was promoted to an Executive position. For some strange reason, being promoted into such a powerful position changed her. Or it really showed what type of person she was. When we all were

supervised by Sarah, she was cool, laid back and down to earth.
When she was promoted into the Executive role she started
having new friends and became a manager that preferred
favoritism and people who kissed ass. I understand that you can't
be as relaxed when promoted but she altered her morals and
ethics. I had too many credentials to kiss anyone's ass, so I was
seen as a threat. There was a position that became open and even
though it was going to be a lateral move, it would have given me
the experience that I needed to move into Executive
Management, in the future. But for some strange reason, I didn't
get it. The new positions that were posted were *given* to
employees that were favorites and everyone was upset with the
decision. It caused employee morale to plummet and it was the
talk/gossip of the day!

Koilya & Tonya's Conversation

Pierce, Tonya
How did they pick those people 4 the
positions...1 in particular has not been in
this department that long...we need 2 talk
ASAP...u can call me anytime after 9pm

Privil, Koilya
I WILL call u today!
I am leaving the company

Pierce, Tonya
What?!

Privil, Koilya
```
Not because of that but because of how
corrupt the management is here
And I really need more money
But that whole thing was wrong how it was
done
```

Pierce, Tonya
```
I c that from the list
Do u still have my cell#?
```

Privil, Koilya
```
Yes mam
```

Pierce, Tonya
```
K, talk 2 u 2nite
```

Tonya was an older woman that sat right across from me. She was very reserved and I admired her because she had a little boy (just like me) and would always talk to me about life and spiritual things. We connected and our connection turned into more than just being co-workers.

Koilya's & Nakeba's Conversation

Blank, Nakeba
```
Hey Gurl
```

Privil, Koilya
```
Hey
```

Blank, Nakeba
They still ain't told me nothing...one of the
managers just IM me doe

Privil, Koilya
What's up?

Blank, Nakeba
Said she gone talk to me in like 10 mins...

Privil, Koilya
Well hopefully it's good news

Blank, Nakeba
I'm like aww snap

Privil, Koilya
Just BE COOL

Blank, Nakeba
Chile please...I doubt it

Privil, Koilya
Just be cool
4real

Blank, Nakeba
Ok I will try...

Fifteen minutes later

Privil, Koilya
So what happened?

Blank, Nakeba
I didn't get it

Privil, Koilya

It's all good
Did they say y

Blank, Nakeba

Yes they said you interviewed very well,
you are a leader and you have all the
skills you just don't have enuff
experience...what da heezy?!!!

Privil, Koilya

Lol ☺
Even from your previous role?

Blank, Nakeba

Girl I ain't stunning dat B.S. cuz dats
what it is...some b.s.

Privil, Koilya

Tru

Blank, Nakeba

When that email got put out they didn't say
nothing about you had to be in the
department for such and such amount of time
They said qualifications!!!

Privil, Koilya

Right
They choose who they want in certain
positions

Blank, Nakeba

So don't give me that "you don't have enuff
experience" B.S. man
Just say you got your picks
Come on now

Privil, Koilya
Right
But they are going to lose all of their
good people

Blank, Nakeba
I had not one, but 3 letters of
recommendations

Privil, Koilya
Because I am out
I am looking for jobs right now as we speak

Blank, Nakeba
And one of them was from the VP of the
department I used to work in
I don't know man
Then they say don't give up, you are doing
a good job, you got what we looking for its
just dat you don't have enuff experience. I
just cried man because its not fair
I'm cool doe

Nakeba was a hot mess! She just came into the department like
six months prior and she thought she deserved one of the
positions. She was ghetto and I have always learned that you
keep the ghetto chics on your side. I spoke to her because she was
cool and if I needed the hook up on a bag, or just the inside
scoop, she was my source. I've never been the type to turn my
nose up at certain people because we all come from different
walks of life. I always would hit it off with the ghetto girls. You
have to keep one of them on your team just in case something

crazy goes down. But she wasn't ready for that role. I was just trying to see what they told her as to why she didn't get it.

Koilya & Sharise's Conversation

Privil, Koilya
What's up?

House, Sharise
Nothing much
Not too many clients today
It seems like it may be a better day

Privil, Koilya
Yeah
It gives me a chance to look for jobs
Peace up A town down

House, Sharise
Exactly. Thanks for the reminder
Lol ☺
Two step

Privil, Koilya
Lol ☺
Lol ☺
Girl
It's all good
This is only a test
And we gotta pass the test that come along
in life

House, Sharise
What doesn't kill us makes us stronger

Privil, Koilya
Right

But baby….
When the blessings start to flow...
None of this will matter

House, Sharise
I think this maybe that time where I'm
forced to make a change and stop breezing
thru things

Privil, Koilya
Right
Me 2

House, Sharise
Remember that dream you had?
About me being scared to jump over the
ditch or something like that, maybe this is
it...I can't be scared to take a risk

Privil, Koilya
I remember
I ain't never scared
Lol ☺
I am a risk taker
You never know if you don't try

House, Sharise
Soldier

Privil, Koilya
Soldierette

House, Sharise
Lol ☺
Northside has some positions

Privil, Koilya
I don't have any health experience

House, Sharise
No, they are office jobs
Billing and stuff

Privil, Koilya
You have to know medical terms though

House, Sharise
Great hours

Privil, Koilya
What's the pay going to be; you think more
or less?

House, Sharise
Not really...go to the site and search office
professional
I don't know and I don't care

Privil, Koilya
U Gotta care
When u have bills

House, Sharise
I know but I gotta get a Monday-Friday
schedule
If I have to take a step back to go
forward, I'll do that

Privil, Koilya
Tru
You have little people to take care of

House, Sharise
I know....little crumb snatchers

Privil, Koilya
Lol ☺
Peter is mean.

I can see that he is going to protect you
when he gets older

House, Sharise
He is better now
He is so happy now
He's just learning to roll over
Some of those little outfits that you gave
me from AJ are too tight

Privil, Koilya
Lol ☺
Give them away
Goodwill
Anybody

House, Sharise
I will
My friend is having a baby in June
You blessed me so I must pass it on

Privil, Koilya
Ahh...

House, Sharise
I think I could admit patients that would
be cool

Privil, Koilya
It's a gravy little desk job

House, Sharise
How about my resume mysteriously
disappeared off of my home space...
Can you help me put one together?
I have a skeleton copy

Privil, Koilya
Send me what u have

Give me until 11am

House, Sharise
Ok
They have great benefits

Privil, Koilya
I know they do...That's the hospital

House, Sharise
Yeah they are in competition with the
banks...
I finally became approved for Childcare
reimbursement

Privil, Koilya
That's good...

House, Sharise
I am ready to go
You talked to Karla
I hope she was straight today

Privil, Koilya
No
I haven't talked to her
Was she supposed to be here?

House, Sharise
Naw she has school
And she had to take that test for another
job

Privil, Koilya
Ooohh ok

House, Sharise
I want to do something since her last day
is tomorrow

Any ideas?

Privil, Koilya
Um...Balloons
Cake
Ice cream

House, Sharise
Yea that will work
I was thinking since she likes to eat (like
me) maybe we can bring some finger foods
like wings and chips

Privil, Koilya
Yeah, wings, cake, and ice cream
Oh yeah and balloons

We all were tired of the drama within the department and Karla

was just a little more focused on finding another job. Karla knew

if she didn't get another job, she would probably have gotten

terminated for being tardy so she was a little more diligent and

finally was hired with another company. Someone got out of the

hell hole!

Privil, Koilya
What do u want your resume to say?

House, Sharise
Just my skills
I'm trying to stay in Investments or
Banking

Privil, Koilya
The final resume is the better one
So what I am going to do is send you my
resume and you can copy and paste what you
want and then I can edit whatever you
include

House, Sharise
Ok
We had our departmental meeting without the
supervisor and it was awful

Privil, Koilya
Really
What happened?

House, Sharise
Later
What time you get off?
Is AJ back from Florida?

Privil, Koilya
He's been back
I get off at six

House, Sharise
I didn't see him at day care

Privil, Koilya
He should be there when you pick Peter up
I'll call you when I get off
Who is your supervisor?
Did u see that list!

House, Sharise
A mess

Privil, Koilya
LJ
Nickelman
Jessica is nasty…And isn't friendly at all!

House, Sharise
I have to call u ASAP at 6:05 PM
This place never ceases to amaze me
Talk to you later
Make sure you answer your phone!

Koilya & Sharlene's Conversation

March, Sharlene
Hey Honey

Privil, Koilya
Hey Chica
It's pretty steady today

March, Sharlene
I see
Just until the later crews come in
Yeah
I am already blowed

Privil, Koilya
Not me…I am looking for another job!

March, Sharlene
Well its no point for me because I AM going
to sell houses soon

Privil, Koilya
I feel you…
But for me, until I can do what I want to
be doing I need to be hustling looking for
another job

March, Sharlene
I do understand that

Privil, Koilya
That is going to compensate me

March, Sharlene
I have some gossip but you can't say anything

Privil, Koilya
Cool

March, Sharlene
Come over when you take your next break

Privil, Koilya
Ok

March, Sharlene
What time are you taking it?

Privil, Koilya
12:30PM

March, Sharlene
Ok
I am so sick of these dumb managers and supervisors
All ignorant

Privil, Koilya
It doesn't surprise me 1 bit

March, Sharlene
Do you know they went into a meeting today with my colleagues and tried to act like they weren't getting any information about

the associates that are not making
appointments with their clients?
Girl now I gotta do all this unnecessary
stuff
If I wasn't trying to leave I am now b/c I
am going to end up saying something to
Sarah fake ass!

Privil, Koilya
Which Sarah?
The head of KA&SC click?

March, Sharlene
Yes

Privil, Koilya
Nasty heifer

March, Sharlene
Girl
I am so mad my head hurts

Privil, Koilya
U don't have to tell me
I know first hand
Don't get mad though

March, Sharlene
I am because it makes it seem like I am not
doing my job

Privil, Koilya
Yeah
But you know better

March, Sharlene
My manager hasn't said anything, but that
is how I feel

Privil, Koilya
Right
All this is, is a test

March, Sharlene
I know

Privil, Koilya
U have to pass them in order to advance

March, Sharlene
And I am going to pass

Privil, Koilya
Me 2
Because baby
When the blessings start to flow…

March, Sharlene
If my manager doesn't tell me to do certain
things, then it doesn't get done
And I am going to take the Real Estate
License test on 06/01
Nothing else needs to be said…and I will
pass

Privil, Koilya
Claim it

March, Sharlene
Because I gotta get out of here

Privil, Koilya
oKAY. I am still applying for different
jobs…Did you get that list?

March, Sharlene
List of what?
Oh the email

Let me look
I can see Dlove

Privil, Koilya
Me2
But Nickelman
She is nasty
She don't even speak
I can't see Lisa Queseda

March, Sharlene
And Jessica

Privil, Koilya
Or
Angelica

March, Sharlene
She was already doing some of the work that
Senior Client Managers do

Privil, Koilya
Jessica is super nasty

March, Sharlene
I told you she would get it

Privil, Koilya
And DJ girly acting ass

March, Sharlene
Some of these people have been job
shadowing for Sarah

Privil, Koilya
It doesn't matter; it's not fair

March, Sharlene
I knew they would give it to him
Because he has applied for everything else

Privil, Koilya
GIVE...
Positions are earned

March, Sharlene
I can't believe Nicole Chauncey didn't get
it
The only person I can see is DLove

Privil, Koilya
Crazy people

March, Sharlene
Angelica did an assignment for Sarah too

Privil, Koilya
I can see 3 of the people that got it,
getting it

March, Sharlene
I agree

Privil, Koilya
U can't even get into Job Shadowing without
Sarah's approval
It's not fair

March, Sharlene
I know

Privil, Koilya
But it's all GOOD...like Lil Kim says

March, Sharlene
Yeah

Privil, Koilya
They ain't getting no $$$

March, Sharlene
The leads may
But no more than $1000

Privil, Koilya
Probably not even that

March, Sharlene
No

Privil, Koilya
God said they won't pimp u

March, Sharlene
Yeah

Privil, Koilya
What's 4 me is 4 me…same as with u

March, Sharlene
I am going to Sabrina at 12:30PM
I am leaving early
U know you sent me an email by accident

Privil, Koilya
I meant to send that to myself

March, Sharlene
Want me to send it back

Privil, Koilya
No
I've sent it to my home email

March, Sharlene
I did too

Privil, Koilya
```
4what
```

March, Sharlene
```
I sent it to your home email
Smart tail
```

Privil, Koilya
```
Oh...
Lol ☺
```

March, Sharlene
```
U gone make me beat you
```

Privil, Koilya
```
We work in different departments
U can't catch me!
```

March, Sharlene
```
I will come over there
```

Privil, Koilya
```
Hurry up...I am about to be out
```

March, Sharlene
```
I am not coming now...Meet you in the hall
though
```

Privil, Koilya
```
Ok
```

Sharlene was my friend. We became really close after Karla left the company. For some reason we just clicked. She was ghetto as all get out but when it came to her job, you would never know that she was a rachet, I will beat your ass chic. She knew how to turn it off and on. We were alike in many ways because I knew how to be professional. But when I had to be Kiki (my alter ego), I was her and she was beginning to have a mind of her own because I was smoking weed like they were cigarettes. I was stressed and the weed would suppress the feelings and issues that I needed to deal with. Especially after Vegas almost was murdered. It was really getting out of control and at this point, I was addicted. I justified my habit and Vegas being my supplier didn't make it any better. Sharlene being my smoking buddy didn't make it any better either.

****

April 29, 2005

Merredith, Kinsasha
Hello, how are you today?
I am great
How r u?

Privil, Koilya
I am fine Queen
What's going on with u?

Meredith, Kinsasha
I talked to my cousin...she told me to tell you to go online and look at the jobs you are interested in...once you find one submit it ASAP

Privil, Koilya
Go online where
Girl
I gots to get out of here
I thought Sarah was cool

Meredith, Kinsasha
Ha ha
Yeah right

Privil, Koilya
But she is trying to hold a sista back!
Girl I was so heated yesterday!

Meredith, Kinsasha
Let me get the correct address so you can
apply

Privil, Koilya
I wasn't really mad but very disappointed
Because they had no real explanation on y
they didn't hire me for the job

Meredith, Kinsasha
I have a client...hold one sec

Privil, Koilya
So I'll take my education and experience
else where

Meredith, Kinsasha
Hey girl, sorry about that...I agree with you
go higher than you can go...they only let
certain people up the ladder in here...if you
know what I mean

Privil, Koilya
Yeap...thanks Queen I appreciate that

Meredith, Kinsasha
My cousin also said that the position you
should apply for are the financial
positions because of your experience

Privil, Koilya
Ok. Girl!!!
I am getting excited looking at the pay!

Meredith, Kinsasha
Good
I heard that it was the bomb...but really try
to get on the school board side...
They make more money
Privil, Koilya
Ok
So if I send you the job numbers, you will
give it to her

Meredith, Kinsasha
I can ask her what's the next step, but she
said go ahead and fill out the info...I will
also ask her who the hiring managers are
for the positions

Privil, Koilya
It has everything on it
So I'll take it from there
Thanks again

Meredith, Kinsasha
Ok I will talk to her again this week...she
went out of town today

Privil, Koilya
Ok
Well I will talk to you later...thank U!

Queen actually started to change. According to the grapevine,
Queen and Randy were being watched and when the police
raided their home, they took everything, even Randy to jail.

Queen didn't come into work for like two weeks because she was incarcerated. After Randy went to jail, Queen's whole attitude changed. She was a totally different person. It's like the two weeks that she had to actually sit and think was her opportunity to get it together. Queen was living in Randy's shadow way to long. She evolved and finally became courageous, inspirational, and unstoppable. A Corporate Chic in her own right. She started dressing better and her self-esteem was in check. Personally, being her neighbor and work confidant, I was proud of her. Its amazing how one person can make another feel so bad about who they are. My preacher always says that God orders stops and steps. His sole purpose is to develop you in a problem. And anytime something increases in one area there is a decrease in another. This was clearly evident with Queen. Queen needed that lock down to get her life together. She even was looking out for me concerning a job. I had a really bad habit of talking about people, so I had to stop talking about her because at the end of the day she was a good person with issues. And hell, who am I to judge?

****

April 30, 2005

Alexander, Kali
Hey what's up?

Privil, Koilya
Hey miss lady
Girl the clients are off the chain today!
Explain your b-day weekend to me

Because Karla and I are trying to plan and
we don't know what you are doing...I know u
were going to Alabama, but tell me dates
and time when you will be gone and when u
want to have the BBQ

Alexander, Kali
Girl you know me...
I don't know
I'm going to Alabama Friday...probably come
back Sunday...we can BBQ Sunday...or Monday
I want to go to Body Tap
But I think they close at 3AM and that is
early

Privil, Koilya
Very...
Um
Let me take some appointments and see what
I can suggest
Where did u want to have it?

Alexander, Kali
Maybe Scores...somewhere cheap
Not too expensive
What about Slice?

Privil, Koilya
Wait
Where do you want to have the party and
list the date
Where do you want the BBQ?

Alexander, Kali
Sunday
May 27th
Since everyone is off Monday
We can have the BBQ at my mother's I guess
I don't have any where else to have it

Privil, Koilya

Do u want to have it at your momma house?
Because I can get the club house at my
community

Alexander, Kali

I don't care...it doesn't bother me...my mother
is pretty cool...she get on my nerves...but she
is cool

Privil, Koilya

Well
Let me know definitely...
So we can plan here...

Alexander, Kali

I might see if I can have a party at
Crucial!

Privil, Koilya

I am trying to plan the BBQ Miss Lady

Alexander, Kali

Oh okay

Privil, Koilya

We will worry about the party in a minute

Alexander, Kali

Okay momma

Privil, Koilya

Lol ☺
I gots to do this
U looked out for me
But I don't need u changing your mind about
having it at your mom's

So let me know because that club house is
really nice
I never had a chance to use it
But u can use it
It is nice in there

Alexander, Kali
Right I will have a place by the end of the
week...you will just have to keep me to it

Privil, Koilya
But if you want to do it at your mom's we
can run it like that

Alexander, Kali
I don't care either way...I need to make a
list of people to invite

Privil, Koilya
Good. So you shouldn't have anything to say
about where "we" are throwing your party
And give me the list by the end of the
week...emails, addresses, or ph#...
We are going to have Fun that weekend

Alexander, Kali
I have 35 people so far
I just don't want my ghetto friends tearing
up anything out there

Privil, Koilya
No girl
Don't worry about that
U want to come by and see the clubhouse
first?

Alexander, Kali
I don't care what it looks like...you know
I'm ghetto...as long as we got drinks and

somewhere to sit...turn on some music ...it's a party!

So Hard to Be...

It's so hard for a girl like me to be who YOU want me to Be.

Pain is an element of being sad.

But the door to happiness is always open.

Why won't I just walk through it?

To be happy you must understand your purpose.

Your purpose is your destiny, your talent, your gift.

I know that right now I am lost and can't find my way.

In this moment,

All I can do is be me and not the person I was designed to be.

So my explanation to you is:

That is why it's so hard for me to be me...or the person that I am supposed to be.

TNG

Each betrayal begins with trust. -**Phish**

Chapter 4:
Betrayal

Betrayal is about learning not to idealize external sources.
–Linda Talley

I know one thing...don't ever say what you will NEVER do.
~Koilya Privil

May 16, 2005

March, Sharlene
Hey honey...
Whats up?

Privil, Koilya
Hey girl
What's good?

March, Sharlene
Chilling...
What training are you about to go into?

Privil, Koilya
Programming for Client Managers

March, Sharlene
Did you make it to work on time?

Privil, Koilya
Yes-mam

March, Sharlene
Good

Privil, Koilya
I told u I am not late to work anymore!
Thank U very much!
Lol ☺

March, Sharlene
Are you coming to my house on Sunday?

Privil, Koilya
I am going to try but I am meeting a
homeboy from Lyrical Writers &
Bloggers...he said that he is going to help
me start doing some things concerning
writing
He wants to meet on Sunday

March, Sharlene
Ok but I am planning on eating around 5 or
6

Privil, Koilya
AJ is leaving so I am coming over

March, Sharlene
Make sure you do
I saw this open mic that people were
reciting poetry on Channel 25 a couple
nights ago
I am trying to look it up so I can find out
how you can get on it

Privil, Koilya
4real?

March, Sharlene
Yeah

Privil, Koilya
I need to start getting practice

March, Sharlene
But the info was going so fast that I
couldn't get all of it
So I will have to sit there until I find it

Privil, Koilya
Ok
Girl this boy is texting me like whoa!

March, Sharlene
Have you talked to him?

Privil, Koilya
Yeap
What's a girl to do?

March, Sharlene
I knew you would

Privil, Koilya
No u didn't

March, Sharlene
I knew you would
because you like him
just make sure you watch him
we don't need unnecessary drama

Privil, Koilya
I know
It will be a secret between me and him
I can't help it

March, Sharlene
So how far are you going?

Privil, Koilya
There is something about him

March, Sharlene
You know what I mean

Privil, Koilya
I know

March, Sharlene
So you are?

Privil, Koilya
No!
Goodness!!!

March, Sharlene
You will never get rid of him

Privil, Koilya
If I do *that*

March, Sharlene
He's already whipped off of a kiss

Privil, Koilya
Lol ☺
Lol ☺
Lol ☺
U think?
I am too if that's the case

March, Sharlene
Just look at what is happening

Privil, Koilya
I know
It's getting worse

March, Sharlene
Terrible

Privil, Koilya
Stop—

March, Sharlene
So what are you going to do?

Privil, Koilya
Saying that!
I don't know…

March, Sharlene
I didn't mean it like that…
Crazy

Privil, Koilya
I keep asking God for strength because I am
weak 4 old boy

March, Sharlene
Ok
But keep in mind that ring stands in the
way of a lot

Privil, Koilya
Exactly

March, Sharlene
Otherwise it would change a lot and you
don't know it, but your ring may be coming
soon now that Vegas is suspecting something

Privil, Koilya
I don't know if I want a ring

March, Sharlene
This may wake him up

Privil, Koilya
Look at what I am doing and I am not even
married!

March, Sharlene
But you haven't done anything except have a
conversation

Privil, Koilya
I know...

March, Sharlene
That is why I don't want you to let it get
to far... and you only feel like that b/c you
don't know where you stand with Vegas

Privil, Koilya
It just seems like if Vegas gets his s***
all the way together, I may bounce
I think I have been looking for a way to
leave...

March, Sharlene
Yeah and that is what is feeding into these
feelings for this guy
You need to sit down and really look in
your heart

Privil, Koilya
Naw...
Sharlene
This Negro has some business about himself
I am going to let you listen to one of the
conversations and let you make your
determination then

March, Sharlene
What do you mean business?

Privil, Koilya
For example…
The boy that sits over there by you is
cute, and I was definitely interested

March, Sharlene
Right

Privil, Koilya
But he had no conversation
There wasn't anything intriguing about him
except his looks, his swag, and his style

March, Sharlene
Right

Privil, Koilya
This dude right here is everything u could
want in a relationship

March, Sharlene
But—

Privil, Koilya
Well he is the type of guys that I like
But…he is married with 3 kids

March, Sharlene
Exactly!
Keep in mind the obstacle
And that is the reason I don't want you to
get to attached

Privil, Koilya
I said *if* his situation gets better then
it's nothing...I would fool around with him
without thinking twice

March, Sharlene
The only reason I want you to be *cautious*
is because when you think about the
situation between them, he should have left
a long time ago
It has been 5 years

Privil, Koilya
Tru…it is cheaper to keep her
Can you say spousal support…
And Child support for 3 kids

March, Sharlene
And you don't know how many times he has
done this too her
She may have done it to him as well but you
don't need to get in the middle

Privil, Koilya
Right…It is nothing but drama

March, Sharlene
He is a good dude to talk to and have
around but just don't take it to far
I am only telling you this to spare your
feelings

Privil, Koilya
Unnecessary drama

March, Sharlene
Yeah…
But you can still find somebody like him
out there

Privil, Koilya
I know one thing...don't ever say what you
will *never* do!

March, Sharlene
And that doesn't mean you have to stay
w/Vegas until you do
U can never say never about anything

Privil, Koilya
Because I said I would *never* live with a
guy
I also said I would *never* mess with a
married man!

March, Sharlene
Technically you are not messing with him
Just talking
And as long as you don't take it *there* you
are fine
But as your best friend I just want you to
take into account your feelings
I Don't want to see you hurt for nothing
In that case I will then have to get
involved

****
Later that day...

March, Sharlene
What are you doing?

Privil, Koilya
Nothing

March, Sharlene
Waiting on this stupid meeting
How did your departmental meeting go?

Privil, Koilya
Good...We had pizza and cake
2 things I don't need

March, Sharlene
I am going to get me a slice for lunch

Privil, Koilya
Go & get a slice from my supervisor

March, Sharlene
No
I am going to the mall for lunch
And today will be my last day going out

Privil, Koilya
My supervisor has a whole box of pepperoni
left

March, Sharlene
My boyfriend and I are going out to lunch...
Sambrinos

Privil, Koilya
Are they good?

March, Sharlene
Yeah...Really good
You need to stop calling that boy on your
break b/c you were late for your
appointment
And that is one of the things that could
have stopped you from getting that position

Privil, Koilya
Ok
Dang

March, Sharlene
I wasn't yelling at you
Just trying to keep you on track

Privil, Koilya
I know

March, Sharlene
So what type of decorations are you getting
for AJ's birthday party?

Privil, Koilya
Thomas the Train

March, Sharlene
Ok...So you want me there by 1 or 2 in the
afternoon

Privil, Koilya
It doesn't matter
It's going to be really informal
I am not stressing about a birthday party
for a one year old

March, Sharlene
Well you still have to decorate, pick up
the cake, and cook
So I know you need me

Privil, Koilya
Yeah...But I am off tomorrow
So I am trying to do everything tomorrow

March, Sharlene
Have you placed the order for the cake?

Privil, Koilya
I am getting the cake from Sam's or Publix

March, Sharlene
Have you already ordered or do you have to
order it?

Privil, Koilya
I have to order it
I will do that tonight

March, Sharlene
So that way it will be ready on Saturday

Privil, Koilya
Right

March, Sharlene
I thought you were off Friday

Privil, Koilya
I am

March, Sharlene
Tomorrow is Thursday

Privil, Koilya
Dang
Girl even my days are all mixed up

March, Sharlene
I am glad I said something

Privil, Koilya
I would have came to work
It just seems like my days are crazy and
all mixed up

March, Sharlene
I understand

Privil, Koilya
No u don't momma...Girl

March, Sharlene
What's wrong?

Privil, Koilya
But I am not stressing about it anymore
It's nothing...

March, Sharlene
Yes you are...
I can tell
What's up?
Be honest

Privil, Koilya
Nothing—just
I don't like this whole situation because
it seems like I really don't have any self-
control

March, Sharlene
Well you have to make yourself have it and
believe me
I have been there
Remember I was telling you about the boy I
met 6 months after me and Brandon started
dating

Privil, Koilya
Right

March, Sharlene
And I talked to that boy for over 3 years

Privil, Koilya
He wasn't married

March, Sharlene
And could not stop myself
Right but it's sort of the same situation

Privil, Koilya
That's the BIG problem I have

March, Sharlene
Well it's a little different
My bad

Privil, Koilya
I wouldn't want anyone to do that to me

March, Sharlene
And you need to find a way to work it out
to where you are not press so you don't get
hurt
...and hate to say it but if you can't you
need to leave him alone
...and I know it's hard to do but you will
save yourself a lot of pain in the end

Privil, Koilya
I know

March, Sharlene
Look at the drama that is already unfolding

Privil, Koilya
Exactly...
I'll work it out

March, Sharlene
And if he is slipping like this now imagine
what would happen if it went further
And that girl might be crazy (not saying *we*
won't give her the business) but she might
be like the women on Cheaters

You know about Cheaters (the show) having people followed and phone conversations taped?
I am going a bit far…
I know

Privil, Koilya
Yeap…
But that's tru
That is what I am constantly thinking about…
I'll be alright

March, Sharlene
Yeah

Privil, Koilya
I can handle this
I am a BIG girl

March, Sharlene
WE will get through this

Privil, Koilya
I do feel like this is a test
Lol ☺
Yeah WE will
See ya momma!

March, Sharlene
Yes
Call me later

Privil, Koilya
Ok

The situation between Vegas and I was just totally out of control. All he would do is smoke weed and spend all of his time with his friends. Our social life was in shambles. It was May 5, 2005 when my whole world was turned upside down. This particular weekend, AJ was spending time with Ann. I completed all of my assignments for class and I wanted to let loose. For about four weeks, there were advertisements boosting the Zab Judah vs. Floyd Mayweather, Jr. fight. Vegas was lounging around *all* day acting undecided about what he wanted to do that night.

That evening as I started to get dressed, he slowly jumped in the shower. I took my time putting on my make-up I made sure every curl was tight with no loose hair. I stood in our walk-in closet acting like I didn't know what I was going to wear. I changed shoes about five times, just so I could see what Vegas was going to do. After about thirty minutes of playing around, I finally put on the outfit that I knew I was going to wear before I started the charade. I already had plans with my co-workers just in case and spoke with Karla while he was in the shower. Just as he was about to leave, I asked him, where he was going. He replied, "To watch the fight." I then asked "where?" He still was pleading the fifth acting like he didn't know. My last question was, "Well, who are going with?" "My homeboys." I then stated, well, I am going with you. He quickly responds, "Koilya, you don't want to be the only girl there. Don't you have plans with the girls from work?" I looked at him long and hard thinking to myself, I am so going to get me a boo thing. I replied, "Yes. I will see you later" and he went his way and I went mine.

I met Karla and Kali at Scores off of Wesley Chapel. I rolled two blunts because I was so through with Vegas. I smoked one before I got in the car and another on the way. Right before I got out of the car, I made sure to place eye drops in my eye, so I wouldn't be turned around at the door for being super high. I also was sure to use my Bath and Body Works hand sanitizer and as I was walking toward the sports bar, I sprayed my Morning Fresh Calgon *Take Me Away* body spray. My cycle came on so I was over cautious. Scores was *packed* that night and the line was long. I went to school with one of the police officers and was able to jump the line. I couldn't believe they were taxing twenty bucks to just to get in when they only paid maybe a $100 for the fight. Businesses in Atlanta got away with charging crazy prices for complimentary services. I shouldn't have to pay to park at an establishment that I am patronizing. Coat check should be a benefit or the business' way of showing quality customer service. Geesh... But this was the place everyone wanted to be on a night like this. Karla and Kali lived on the east side of Atlanta and was waiting on me. I made sure to tell Karla, I wanted a Corona so I wouldn't have to wait forever for my drink. I couldn't take a chance with alcohol with the amount of weed I smoked prior. Every one from the east side of Atlanta was in Scores. My goodness! People were standing all on each other. We were all posted up right next to the bar blabbing about work and who was sleeping with who and how unfair our department had become. Right before the fight, I went to the bathroom because I didn't want to have to worry about leaking or having to pee during the fight. Many couples were booed up; a lot of dikes were in there looking hard as hell ready to turn good straight girls to the other side, and single men and woman were in there looking to hook up with anyone they could take home that night. As I am walking through the crowd, trying to make my way to the bathroom, I saw this guy on his way to men's bathroom trying to grab some ass. Shaking my head, I told myself, I don't want none of that. I never saw his face but I remembered he had on some True Religion Jeans with a Luxe white t-shirt, a fitted cap and some fresh new Jordan's. I finally made it to the bathroom, handled my business, washed my hand, tipped the pushy bathroom lady, primped in the mirror one last time, and made it back to my spot. The fight just started and I loved Zab, so I was rooting for him.

The place was filled with so much noise. I stood there drinking my Corona and I enjoyed the buzz I had. As I am minding my own business, I felt someone tap me on the shoulder. I turn to see who it was, and it was the thirsty guy I saw on the way to the bathroom. What *hell* did *he* want? His face wasn't that bad looking. He was a brown skinned guy without any blemishes or bumps. He had diamonds on his top row and a Movado watch on his wrist. He said, "Could you tell the waitress to get me a

Corona?" I didn't say ok or even respond. I was twisted and just grabbed the waitress and asked for his drink. I was conscious and very aware, but I wasn't really interested. I was *not* in my right mind. I grabbed the waitress for him and was really interested in the game because I loves me some Zab! The guy touched my arm again at the same time saying, how soft my skin was and that he wanted to make sure I ordered the drink because I was closer to the bar. I placed my hand out, not saying a word, so he could give me the money for his drink. Once the transaction was complete, I went back to having a good time not even realizing that Karla was talking to this guy's friend. I didn't know where Kali disappeared to, but I was stuck having to entertain this talkative guy. I finally gave him the Corona and just so he could make conversation, he asked who I wanted to win. Of course I told him Zab and he instantly said, "I hope you aren't a betting woman because Mayweather is going to win this fight." I shook my head, like whatever leave me alone, I am uninterested and he just kept talking. Of course his prediction was right, and Zab lost the fight. The many people that were there started to slowly leave. Within fifteen minutes, the bar was instantly turned into a mini-club scene and we decided to stay there since we paid twenty bucks to get in. Karla cut off all communication with us to talk with some random and I was left entertaining Mr. Ass Grabber. I had to make the best of the situation and casually talked and flirted with him.

The music was blasting and everyone left in the bar/club were wide-open! I finally asked him his name after he finally decided to buy my drink. His name was Troy Davis. I mean really, who introduces themselves with their first and last name? But he did and even though I know I should haven't have been taking shots, I started taking lemon drop shots back to back followed up with Coronas to even everything out. Kali finally reappeared when she saw the *free* drinks being passed around. We were dancing, singing and having a ball with these random guys. When I had an opportunity to look at the clock it was already three o'clock in the morning. We continued to dance and when we finally became tired I allowed Troy to walk me to my car. Kali went ahead and left because evidently she didn't snag her a boo thang and Karla was "booed up" with Troy's friend since the fight. Troy ended up walking me to my car. When we got to the car he started out about how he was so interested and he had never met anyone like me. His teeth was shining and I was so twisted, it didn't matter what he was saying. I just started to kiss him. As I am kissing him, I felt the same butterflies I felt when I used to kiss Vegas. This was weird. So we just kept passionately kissing each other like, we both needed an outlet. We were all over each other like two drunk teenagers. I didn't care about anything; all of the hurt that I was feeling mixed with being high and drunk went into making out with this guy who I knew nothing about.

My period was on so he wasn't going to get my goodies. After about fifteen to twenty minutes of slobbering each other down, I came to my senses and explained a thousand times that this was so - not me. I don't remember getting his number or him getting mine, but I needed to get home because it was almost 6:00 AM in the morning. Vegas knew this was not like me. When I finally got home, and *that was only through God's grace and mercy*, I checked my car thoroughly to make sure there wasn't any evidence of what had happened. But this dude left his hat in my car! I would never see him again so I threw it away. Needless to say, Vegas got home before I walked through the door and he knew my period was in effect so me taking a shower to wash this guys smell off of me, didn't even cross his mind. I washed away my sins for that night thinking that I would never hear from this guy again.

While at work that following Monday, I get this phone call from a strange number; because I was searching for jobs, I thought it was a potential employer. "Good Morning" was my response and the person on the other end then stated, "Good Morning, how are you?" I am confused like hell about the call and I respond very slowly by saying, "I am *f-i-n-e*. Who is this?" the voice then says, "This is Troy, the guy you met at Scores on Saturday." I immediately had to ask, "Did we exchange phone numbers? Because I don't remember too much from that night and please forgive me for being so un-lady like. That is not in my character.

I was twisted and placed myself in a situation that I was not prepared for." Troy started to say, "Shawty, it's all good. We both are adults. There is no need for you to apologize. I am digging your vibe and if I felt like you were just some random female without any morals, I wouldn't have called you. Plus, I have to get my hat from you. I think I left it in your car."

Me being the nervous, Koilya, I apologized again for my actions and explained that I didn't have his hat and I needed to get back to work. He asked if he could call me sometime and I told him it was cool. We talked on my lunch breaks, on the way home from work, and anytime I was away from Vegas. This went on for about two weeks. In two weeks, we were able to sneak away from our situations (his baby momma and my baby daddy) and meet at the Drive through movies, for dinner, and even the Jazz Festival. He told me that he lived with his children's mother and they were going through problems; which was so similar to Vegas and I. But then I received a call from this woman who told me that she was married to Troy. I explained to her that I was unaware and she wouldn't have to worry about me anymore. For some strange reason, I didn't keep my word. I was already hooked to something fresh, new, and what I thought I wanted. This happened within only a month and my feelings (confused as they were) was to the point of no return.

****

To Be Continued…

Acknowledgements

I would first like to give thanks to God for allowing me to be in His will for my life. Expressing and creatively writing brings me so much joy and I know it is a gift because I can get lost in writing and wouldn't have to ever get paid for it. It is truly my therapy and being able to share it with the world is my gift to you. I pray this story not only entertains but it allows you to self-evaluate and correct along the way. By the time you read volume three, I am sure you will be in a place of making new decisions and choices about life or even having a new perspective about things. Being of service is a focused and disciplined journey and you must be able to hear the Voice of God when He speaks to you. When He spoke to me about this project, I listened and was obedient but I was disappointed when I ran out of marketing money. This book was initially written in 2009 but I had no real plan of getting it out to the masses. However, I did receive amazing feedback and that fueled my spirit and made me not want to give up on it. Timing is everything.

I am grateful for my mother, father and two sisters who have supported me in everything from day one. Support is extremely important while trying to birth a dream. No one can see your vision and when you have people believing in you, even when they can't see what you see, it is truly amazing and inspirational for them to cheer for you and not know what they are cheering for.

I am thankful for my ex-husband who was understanding throughout my creative process…the first time…and helping with resources and funding this time. We are forever connected and will always remain friends until death do us part.

I send a warm embrace to Mrs. Moss; my high school English professor. She is the reason I learned to write. She ensured that anything I wrote was perfect and flawless. She brought my talent and gift to life. Ms. Bryant; my creative writing instructor, allowed my mind to explore and helped me to believe that being innovative is endless. I saved all of my creatively written pieces from the tenth grade. (Who does that? A Writer.) Thank you two from the bottom of my heart!

I am appreciative of all of my family, friends, advisors, mentors, and associates who gave me strength through encouragement. I would like to thank Naomi Mance for the initial cover design because it was as if she passed the baton to Jerron Leary who literally looked in my brain and drew what I saw for the cover and the characters in the coloring book. Social Media is a powerful tool. You have to purchase the coloring book for a little girl in your life to learn about how our paths crossed. I am thankful to the ladies of Sisters Striving for Excellence, Inc. When the group was created almost fourteen years ago, I had no idea that the idea would live this long. Thank you to all of the ladies who represent the organization with class, professionalism, and integrity. Thanks to Synovia Dover-Harris, a colleague and the owner of A2Z Books Publishing for providing me an avenue to encourage, inspire and uplift a mass amount of people.

Last but not least, I MUST thank you for picking up this book. If this book is really good and you think that other women should read it…tell them about it. Word of mouth is how the Corporate Chics movement will extend.

About the Author

Tawana Necole is a humanitarian, writer, and entrepreneur. As the Co-Founding President of Sisters Striving for Excellence, Inc., a non-profit, charity-based organization that focuses on the importance of female professional-business development and preparedness for life after college; the book was written to convey a message to women from all walks of life. The author has experienced the corporate world through holding different positions in the banking and retail industry and some of the events in the story is based on real life events. Holding a Bachelor in Business Management, Masters in Business & Organizational Security Management and Project Management, she works as a Management Consultant with her company Corporate Chics Enterprises. She is a native of Wadmalaw Island, a small city in Charleston, SC, but currently resides in Atlanta, GA, with her two boys Chace and Chad.

Resources

The Internet is a powerful and significant tool in technology and in order to build a brand, you must understand how and where to utilize your resources. Here are a few of my resources.

www.CorporateChics.net

www.SistersStrivingforExcellence.org

www.A2ZBooksPublishing.com

Life and its MANY

LESSONS

The Follow Up

By: Tawana Necole

As women we have the responsibility to educate each other. Education teaches the uninformed and the ignorant. The key into understanding the conditions of life is to be responsible for your own actions and behaviors. I had to learn that at a very young age with the death of my brother and father. When knowledge is obtained, it is the accountability of that individual to grow and learn from every encounter life brings.

As a successful woman, I have that opportunity. I have the ability to reach anyone who picks up this book. And because I am liable for the experience that you take from this book, I am going to allow you to walk down this journey called life with me. My journey so far has been unique, intriguing, filled with struggles, and many hardships. The story of love and the sacrifices some people make for true happiness is breath-taking and sometimes undeniably *wrong*. That's why I want to share my lessons, experiences, and thoughts about me and the people who were in my environment or my world when I was going through...

Strategically, my story may reach you to help you *through*. Ladies, in order to leave a legacy, you have to build a BRAND. I had to tell the whole world about my lessons and what I discovered about life. I think it was August Wilson who stated, "*I found out life is hard but it ain't impossible.*" WOMEN are the most powerful human beings in the world, with guidance, knowledge and love. *Smart Women Finish Rich*, as David Bach would say. If you are not a Corporate Chic, you are still some type of woman handling your business. And even if you are not handling your business as you should be, my message to you is to know that you have everything you need to become a successful woman. Success is not just defined by abundance or having money. The true definition is being happy with who you are, what you do, who you are with, and what you have, currently. If you are not at this point in your life, let me be the first to say that God has designed you fully equipped to handle all the challenges that may come your way during your journey to get you to this ultimate goal.

■■

Hindsight knowledge is the most valuable but why does it have to be *hindsight"* Why does it have to be so late? As you can clearly see throughout this entire first volume; I (Koilya P.) clearly missed all of the whispers and ignored all the signs. Now, as a lifetime student of wisdom, knowledge, and understanding, I eventually started learning to never ignore the signs. Say it with me, *"Never ignore the signs. "* We get signs all of the time. As women, love comes easy and we usually love really hard when we are in relationships. Generally once our mind is made up about something, we are satisfied with our decision. But when a man enters the equation, we somehow lose who we are and we never stick to our decision. We all at one point in our lives, have decided to leave a man once we were fed up with him not treating us right, and then two weeks later we are right back in his arms. So let's understand love and decision making.

What is Love?

It is a decision about how we act, even when no one is watching. The dictionary states it is profoundly tender, passionate affection for another person. God is the essence of love. Love is an unselfish loyal and benevolent concern for the good of another. Love sacrifices & lives for others... *A Return to Love* by Marianne Williamson breaks down lessons from the *A Course in Miracles* and she explains that **love is**...and when you love, you should love with your whole heart in the beginning of any type of *ship*. (Relationship, Partnership, Friendship, etc.). She goes on to say that love is not something that should be earned. It is something that is given freely. Have you ever experienced a homeless person begging and everything in you wanted to just give them what they were asking for without knowing them or their situation? Forget that he/she may spend whatever you decide to donate to booz or crack. The fact that you gave without knowing that person's situation demonstrates your Love for them when you don't even know their name. That is an act of Love and it demonstrates what or how we should treat one another in this dimension of life.

Decision Defined

A decision is a determination after consideration. It is coming to a conclusion and cutting off other options. All decisions have consequences: present or eternal. Consequences are built into your decisions & your actions. You will never change what you are not willing to confront. Excluding communication, these two components {love and decisions} are vital in relationships.

Putting it All Together

When a woman is in a loving relationship, there is no doubt about the feelings for her significant other. Everything is reciprocal. A relationship is balanced when two people love each other unconditionally. When you question if someone really loves you, that's when you have made a mistake in the decision of loving someone. I know it's hard to let go of someone that you care about, however, when you love yourself more than anyone besides God, you are able to make sound quality decisions. So if you haven't made good decisions about relationships, this is where your answers lie.

Questions to Ponder

If you place yourself second, why would a man/woman place you first? You have to love all of you first. Your short coming, your weakness, your strengths, your nose, your fat..love you.

If you disregard your qualifications or settle for someone, why should the person that you settle for treat you with the love you deserve? Never settle or be shallow. There should always be virtue qualities in a significant other but be wise enough to pay attention to actions and if they are being reciprocated.

If you don't love yourself enough to consider the importance of self-love and self-perseverance, why would you receive it in return from someone? The Law of Attraction is real. Energy is real. And we receive what we give.

Have you ever stopped to think that sometimes you are the reason for the misfortunes that you experience?

As people, we are given everything we need for this journey in life. Most times we choose to ignore our intuition. You cannot afford to if you want to experience a purposeful, prosperous life.

Moving toward the Future
Now that you have been enlightened and somewhat understand what it means to love; it's time to get out of toxic relationships that you have been a part of for convenience. Sometimes to be better we must get out and walk away! I have learned that I cannot change people when I want them to change. I cannot save people, I can only love them; even if it's from afar. They will

only change when they are ready and receptive.

Five Simple Steps to Assist with Love & Decision Making
1. Love God with all your heart and all your soul.
2. Walk in Love. Meaning always set out to do something good for someone. Be a peacemaker.
3. Be in love with yourself.
4. Never settle for someone who is not on the same level as you spiritually, mentally, or emotionally.
5. Don't ignore the signs that tell you BEWARE.

The POWER of love and the POWER of desire are magnetic. I receive inspiration from many different avenues. Movies aren't only interesting, engaging, and intriguing, but because I am an artist in many different aspects, I love everything about that particular expression and the impression that it leaves on others. Of course the plot of the story line has to be extremely exceptional, but when you have great actors to pull of the story, that makes it even better.

One of my favorite movies hands down is *Slum Dog Millionaire*. The movie depicts the journey of a kid that grew up in India. When I say he was dealt a terrible hand when it came to life, it's an understatement. Jamal (the main character) lived in poverty and his mother was murdered forcing him into homelessness. His brother was the Judas of his life, but even though he experienced many misfortunes, his desire and love for this one woman allowed him to win the game of life.

The power of love and desire is amazing and it is the SECRET to life. It is the simplest concept to grasp when it comes to getting in line with the Universe. The movie begins with Jamal as the guest on a very popular game show, "Who wants to be a Millionaire?"

Jamal's experiences assisted him in winning an abundance of money and his one true love. What is so amazing about the book turned flick, is the fact that he didn't want to really win the game. This was an attempt to reconnect with Latika (Rubina Ali) his love interest in the movie. The money just became a great incentive. That's the bases of the plot and story. AND that is why the moral and the movie is so intriguing. Experiences are usually a great testimony and ministry. **Understand** that your experiences, usually lead to encouragement and empowerment: the three essential components Corporate Chics is built upon.

Love is unconditional. The starting point in *Napoleon Hill's* book "Think and Grow Rich" is Desire. Wishes are desires with the ability to become Definite. Something is not a wish once you act upon it. DESIRE CAN BE TRANSLATED INTO REALITY. Jamal believed with his all that he would win back, his one true love. He chose a definite goal and placed all his energy, all his willpower, all his effort and did everything to back that goal. And it became a reality.

Have you ever heard of **The Secret**? Well, if you haven't, I love spreading knowledge and this is something you must know and understand in order to get anything you want in life. **The Secret** reveals the most powerful law in the Universe. "The knowledge of this law has run like a golden thread through the lives and the teachings of all the prophets, seers, sages and saviors in the world's history, and through the lives of all truly great men and women. All that they have ever accomplished or attained has been done in full accordance with this most powerful law. By applying the knowledge of this law, you can change every aspect of your life. This is the secret to prosperity, health, relationships and happiness. This is the secret to life." (*The Secret,* Rhonda Byrne).

There you go! The movie provides a significant philosophy and simple principle. Hope, faith, tolerance, and courage were the components, Jamal utilized to achieve his goal of becoming a millionaire and winning his one true love. View the movie if you haven't seen it.

Information is quotations found on www.secret.tv/

Anything you give up to better your relationship with God reaps GREAT harvests & benefits. But sometimes we are oblivious to the signs. We sleep walk through life not paying attention. Paying attention to everything that happens in your life or around you is your real job. Pay attention to your life and the messages that it is telling you. Becoming poisoned with so many negative influences, especially with the media controlling how, what and who is influential, is practically the reason we all should be cognizant of what we are thinking and what we are learning. Normally, *the signs* are a quiz or a test to see if you are paying attention or if you are in-tune with you. If this is not the case, as it was in my situation, you will be poisoned.

Poison comes in many forms....and the things that were screaming at me were loud and clear. The media has the ability to influence a mass amount of people. But most of the shows or information that is being reported is senseless, bias, opinionated, and untrue. POISON.

I am truly convinced that this is our society's cancer. Poison and toxins that drown out that voice, is reasoning. It confuses you. As soon as you begin to feel confused, that is a sign that it is not the real you....it's not the something that effortlessly guides you. That *something told me to or not to* is your compass. It is your invisible satellite; you're GPS. It's a soft gentle voice. It's never overbearing. It is a complete gentleman. In the spiritual world, it is called the Holy Spirit. (Some information compiled from Oprah's Life Class).

God grant me the serenity to accept the people I cannot change, the courage to change the one I can...and the wisdom to know it's me. ~ Unknown

The only person over whom you have direct and immediate control is yourself. The most important assets to develop, preserve and enhance, therefore are your own capabilities. And no one can do it for you—YOU must cultivate the habits of leadership effectiveness for yourself —and doing so will be the single BEST investment you'll ever make! ~ **Steven R. Covey**

■■
Life Lesson I

"One important life lesson that I will never forget is when people develop and mature, they must change in their development process." –**Koilya Privil**

Interested in Publishing a BOOK??

Visit: www.A2ZBooksPublishing.com

CPSIA information can be obtained at www.ICGtesting.com
Printed in the USA
LVOW10s1042120715

445910LV00003BA/64/P